CAPTIVE AUDIENCE

CAPTIVE AUDIENCE

STORIES

DAVE REIDY

Brooklyn, New York

Printed in the United States of America
10 9 8 7 6 5 4 3 2 1

All the characters in *Captive Audience* are fictional. With a few obvious exceptions, any resemblance to actual events or actual persons—living or dead—is purely coincidental. In pieces in which the author has chosen, for the purposes of creating a fictional story, to use the name of an actual person, the events and dialogue are fictional.

Ig Publishing
178 Clinton Avenue
Brooklyn, NY 11205
www.igpub.com

Library of Congress Cataloging-in-Publication Data

Reidy, Dave.
Captive audience / Dave Reidy.
p. cm.
ISBN 978-0-9815040-4-9
1. Entertainers--Fiction. I. Title.
PS3618.E552C37 2009
813'.6--dc22

2009008211

For my family

CONTENTS

THE REGULAR

Around eight each weeknight, I left work and took the El north to a small club called Whirly Gigs. While roadies and band members wrangled cords and tuned guitars on the club's tiny elevated stage, I sat at the narrow end of the bar, my messenger bag, two-toned cotton sweater, jeans and brown plastic-framed glasses identifying me as a member of the creative proletariat. My stool was the furthest one from the stage. Blasé, aging indie kids ordering drinks often blocked my view, but I didn't care. I could hear everything I needed to see.

Julian held court each night in the booth closest to the stage. Guys who barely knew him would approach and extend their hands for a hipster's handshake, a curled-finger lock, tug, and release. Julian obliged each one coolly. The girls sitting with him communicated interest, excitement, or jaded lust with their eyes. Julian absorbed their attention without courting it. If my look identified me as someone with a job, Julian's sloppy hair, denim jacket, and tub-soaked tight jeans placed him outside the workaday world.

When the first act took the stage, Julian would leave the

adoring courtiers and his stage-side seat for the stool next to mine. One night I asked him why no one ever tried to drag him back to his booth, or pull him into the crowd to dance. He shrugged, and sipped his bourbon. "I put the word out," he said, his eyes on the stage. "During the shows, I listen to the music, and I talk only to you."

I'd been a regular at Whirly Gigs since moving back home from college in 1996. Julian arrived a few years later. I noticed him right away, but didn't speak to him at first—I spoke only to the bartender, Casey, and once he knew enough to give me a bourbon when I sat down, we didn't speak very often.

One night, on his way back from the bathroom, Julian stood next to my stool during the opening act of a three-act bill. The band was aping The Stooges without the punk pioneers' energy or talent, though energy and talent wouldn't have made them sound any better. Distaste was surely visible on my face, but Julian never looked at me. "The snare is peaking too high," he said. His analysis was that of an audiophile, of one who lived for sound and executed unconsciously and crudely what a sophisticated computer program could do electronically and exactly. Julian heard instrument and microphone inputs as visible tracks—jagged peaks above deep, repeating fissures—stacked like a dense, multicolored polygraph display. I could hear the same images in my own head.

From then on, Julian and I analyzed every live set at Whirly Gigs as if it were being recorded. We spoke of sound in terms of two-dimensional images: distorted guitars crying out for compression, backing vocals that needed gating. We weren't friends. We were something less. I'd never seen Julian outside of Whirly Gigs, never spoken to him on the phone, and it seemed, beyond our nightly meeting place, that seeing sound was all we had in common. But that was enough to make sitting alongside Julian the high point of my day.

When the headliners, whoever they were, had played their final encore, Julian would clap me on the back and head back to his booth. I would pay my tab and head for the El. On my walk to the Belmont station, I would pass a karaoke club called Starmakers. Because of its stock in trade, Starmakers—the name alone—was an insult commonly overheard at Whirly Gigs. If a singer's performance was overly earnest or overwrought, one regular might shout "Starmakers" into the ear of another before heading for the bar. To associate an act with karaoke was worse than calling its sound dated, or derivative, or even boring. At Whirly Gigs, "Starmakers" was the atom bomb of on-the-spot reviewing.

Despite the hipsters' disdain, Starmakers was usually packed when I walked past its plate-glass façade. Inside, sleeves were rolled up and collars unbuttoned, and skirts were twisted from repeated shimmies across vinyl benches to visit the bathroom and the bar. In my head, I kept a running tally of the songs I heard on my nightly pass-bys. "I Will Survive" and "Like A Prayer" were favorites, and bachelorette parties often tackled "Girls Just Wanna Have Fun" en masse. But the real treats were the choices that confounded me, like the warbling older woman who performed Janis Joplin's "Me and Bobby McGee" as if it were a Presbyterian hymn, and the guy who gave a pitch-perfect rendering of Michael McDonald's supporting vocals on "This Is It"—a 1979 duet with Kenny Loggins—but declined to sing Loggins' parts, reducing the song's verses to underfed synthesized instrumental breaks. Once I heard—but didn't see—a man singing Captain and Tennille's "Love Will Keep Us Together." What sort of guy, I wondered, would select that song from a binder full of other choices? I promised myself that if ever again I heard a man singing that song, I would get a good look at him and buy him a round. He would deserve it, somehow.

Getting off the El just north of Downtown, near the building where I spent my days working as a senior art director for Fahrenheit Graphic Design, I would walk to the open-air lot where I had parked my car seventeen hours earlier, then drive home to the edge of the city, one of only a handful of Chicago neighborhoods with a zip code that did not begin with 606. Mine was 60707, and when I saw the soccer fields, car dealerships and day-care centers on my stretch of Fullerton Avenue, the 607 seemed about right.

My apartment was in the basement of my parents' house, a duplex with a door in the gangway that allowed me to come and go as I pleased. I had a bedroom just big enough for a twin bed and a dresser, a bathroom with a shower, and a living room with a kitchenette along one wall. The living room doubled as my home studio, which consisted of a Mac G5, a digital mixing board, four top-shelf microphones, and sound-absorbing cotton panels on the walls and ceiling.

Each night, after arriving home from Whirly Gigs, I would stay up until three or four in the morning scouring file-sharing networks for individual tracks of multi-track pop recordings. I imported each song piece by piece—the drums isolated from the bass, the backing vocals separated from the lead—and investigated every hiss or fumble or bleed that caught my eye. Once, I spent two weeks of late nights with The Clash's "Clampdown," searching for the reasons that Joe Strummer's guitar had been buried in the final mix and trying to decide for myself whether or not Topper Headon deserved his "Human Drum Machine" moniker. (He did.) When I had seen all there was to see in a given song, I would return to the networks, poach another masterpiece, and start the process all over again.

This was my life. It was static and less than I wanted, but with my studio, Whirly Gigs, and Julian, it was just enough to live on.

One Monday, I had to work late and didn't arrive at Whirly Gigs until twenty minutes past nine. I found Julian standing next to my regular stool, staring at the stage. By this point in the evening, the stage was usually cluttered with a drum kit, a half-dozen amps and a slithering mass of black cords. Tonight, however, a portable projection screen flanked by two elevated portable speakers occupied the drum kit's usual position. To the left of one of the speakers, a laptop and two microphones rested on a folding table. The front of the stage was barren but for a monitor mounted on a spindly metal tripod and an empty microphone stand.

I dropped my bag between the stool and the bar and glanced at Julian. "Are they doing an open mike night?" I asked, hoping it wasn't so. He didn't say anything. He just kept staring at the stage.

A woman at the bar ordered a dirty martini. The platinum band of her engagement ring was milky in the stage light, and her silk blouse laid neatly on the curve of her left hip. Over her shoulder, two men wearing khakis and golf shirts emblazoned with corporate logos sat in a booth, chatting up two women sitting across from them. The woman closer to the bar wore nylons, black high-heeled pumps, and a gray jacket-and-skirt set. After the guy across from her dribbled beer foam on his shirt, both women erupted in nearly identical cackles.

That was when it hit me. They were sitting in Julian's booth.

Suddenly, Bon Jovi's "Wanted Dead or Alive" blasted from the portable speakers and the projection screen ignited with quick-cut images of Asian men and women riding bicycles, slurping noodle soup, and pruning topiary menageries. A slightly overweight young man wearing a white short-sleeve button-down, blue jeans, and ear-covering headphones was now standing behind the folding table. A wireless mike, protected by black foam shaped like a wrecking ball, was held in front of his mouth by a plastic arm connected to the headphones. He looked like the pilot of a traffic helicopter.

"Welcome," he announced, "to Karaoke Monday at Whirly Gigs."

As Casey put my drink on the bar, I asked him what was going on. He told me that management had been running an ad for "Karaoke Monday" in the *Tribune* for the past two weeks and had stopped booking bands on Mondays. "Management" was a rotating cast of shadowy Serbians, a pair of whom showed up at least once a week in loose, open-collared black shirts and tailored black slacks to let the bartenders and the bouncers know they were watching everything. Since taking over Whirly Gigs a few years ago, the Serbians had twice threatened to convert the club into a hookah lounge. In each instance, a week-long, sold-out residency of local bands made good—Smashing Pumpkins the first time, Wilco the second—had put enough money in the Serbians' pockets to stay the club's execution. Were the Serbians now using karaoke to take Whirly Gigs back from its regulars? Were they trying to turn the place into Starmakers?

"What about the other nights?" I asked.

"Bands," Casey said, "just like before. But with this . . . ." He turned to the stage and his voice trailed off.

"The regulars won't ever come back," I said.

Casey nodded.

When I turned to commiserate with Julian, he was gone.

I grabbed my bag and hurried out to the street. Julian was already a half-block away. I jogged after him, coins and keys jangling noisily in my pockets, and slowed to a walk as I fell in alongside him.

"Where are you going?" I asked.

"I don't know." Julian's clenched jaw and flattened eyebrows were probably supposed to make him look angry, but his wet eyes gave him away.

As we walked along in silence, something soured in my stomach. Whirly Gigs was dying; in a sense, it was already dead. I could find another place to see sound—this was Chicago, after all—but would Julian follow me there? Would sound look the same if he wasn't there to share it?

But Julian's loss was even greater than my own. He was now a king without a country, his throne occupied by consultants who saw Whirly Gigs as a place to sit while they waited their turn at the karaoke mike. Even if Julian decided to find another club and make it his own, he would be nothing more than another good-looking hipster.

We were crossing Racine Avenue against a red light when my mind flashed to a place that could return to us some of what we had lost. When we reached the sidewalk, I grabbed Julian's elbow, stopping his retreat. "Last night I found the individual tracks of Cheap Trick's *At Budokan*."

Julian looked at me as if he hadn't understood. "What?"

"I found the individual recording tracks of Cheap Trick's *At Budokan*."

"You mean each song."

"No. Each track of each song."

He stared at me. "Where did you find them?"

"File sharing," I said. "I've got them all loaded into my computer. Come over to my place. We'll give them a look."

Julian lowered his eyes to my hand, which still held his elbow. I let go, and replayed the previous ten seconds in my head. My mouth went dry as I realized that my proposal had sounded something like a proposition, the audiophile's equivalent of the bachelor's ruse in which he tells a potential conquest that she must see the breathtaking view from his apartment.

Julian began to nod, almost imperceptibly at first. "All right," he said. "Let's go."

As we walked toward the Belmont El station, I assured myself that Julian had understood that I had meant nothing untoward, and if any doubt lingered, I would prove it at my apartment by delivering what I had promised and nothing more. And just when I had managed to put my mind at ease,

I realized that my invitation had left me vulnerable in a way I'd failed to anticipate: what if Julian found out that I lived with my parents?

I led Julian around the side of the house, down the three concrete steps, and inside. I turned on the lamp near the door, but the dim yellow light failed to brighten things up. In that moment, I experienced the space as I thought Julian might have: the trapped aromas of mildew and micro-waved meals, the oak footboard of my twin bed detailed with carvings of dogs and cats, bundled cords emerging from the back of my recording console, untreated wooden stairs leading to the floor above.

I took off my coat, laid it over the footboard, and looked for the bottle of bourbon I'd started the night before.

"Nice place," Julian said.

"Thanks."

I poured bourbon into two coffee mugs and set them down on coasters in front of two rolling chairs. I sat in the better chair, not wanting to make things more awkward by overtly deferring to Julian, and immediately called up the *At Budokan* tracks. I double clicked on the lead-guitar track of "Hello There" and watched the thin, vertical black line move from left to right over the visual representation of the music we heard in the speakers.

"Wow," Julian whispered.

We spent the next three hours analyzing each track of *At Budokan's* first two songs, finishing more than half the bottle of bourbon between us. As the backing vocals of "Come On, Come On" melted into the noise of 14,000 cheering Japanese, Julian said, "Let's stop there. I could look at tracks all night, but I don't want to use them all up, you know?"

My first thought was that Julian was making an excuse to leave, but he poured himself another drink and sat back in his chair. It occurred to me then that in stopping our analysis after only two songs, Julian was creating a reason to come back.

"We don't have to stop if you don't want to," I said. "I've got other albums."

"Track by track?" Julian asked.

I nodded.

"Can I see?" Julian said, leaning forward toward the monitor.

"Sure." I let go of the mouse and Julian took it with his right hand. As I poured more bourbon into my mug, I took stock of the situation. Julian was in my house, on my studio computer, relishing the audio I had collected, showing no sign of leaving and every indication he intended to return. I had lost Whirly Gigs, but had gained something more of Julian. For the first time I could remember, I felt like my life could do more than keep me going: it could fill me up.

Julian scrolled through all my downloaded tracks, his heavy-lidded eyes glowing green in the monitor light. "The Clash," he said with an approving nod. "Blur. Pavement. Nirvana's *In Utero* sessions?"

I nodded.

"The original Albini sessions?"

I nodded again.

"Not sure how you found those," Julian said. "Don't want to know."

I sipped my bourbon. Even if Julian had wanted to know how I got the *In Utero* sessions, I wouldn't have told him.

"Journey?" Julian asked. It looked like he was trying not to sneer.

I felt blood flooding the vessels in my face. I could have played off having Journey in my collection as a hipster's slumming lark, or cited the difficulty of finding any track-by-track recordings on the web—a sort of beggars-can't-be-choosers defense. But the truth was that finding Journey's "Faithfully" had been the culmination of a yearlong search. By coincidences of vocal quality and range, I could sing just like the band's lead singer, Steve Perry.

The previous week, in the privacy of my studio, with my eyes closed and the mike in both hands, I had belted out "Faithfully" with the full band (minus Perry) playing in my headphones. When I was done, I moved my own vocal track, a horizontal, hot pink image of intermittent sound, just below Steve Perry's neon green original and magnified both one-hundred times. At that size, a vocalist's performance looks like impossibly steep summits and unfathomable glacial crevasses between flatlands of silence. I spent an hour comparing the visual representations of the two vocal tracks, noting tiny discrepancies and savoring the fine details of each similarity.

In another situation, the whole thing might have made for a funny story. But given the abomination we had witnessed at Whirly Gigs a few hours before, I had no intention of appearing to be in league with karaoke nation.

"Journey are people, too," I replied, trying to laugh off Julian's question. I took a sip of my drink. When I saw he was still waiting for an explanation, I said, "I was desperate for some new tracks, so I took them. I checked out the drum track and the lead guitar track and called it quits."

Julian opened his mouth in surprise. "You downloaded 'Faithfully' and didn't even give Steve Perry a look?"

As Julian turned back to the monitor with the mouse in his hand, I said, "No! Don't!"

He must have thought I was putting him on, because he smiled and kept going. When he started playback, the neon green vocal track was still silenced. The hot pink vocal track was not.

My voice sounded like Perry's but, unmixed and unmastered, the vocal was obviously not the original. Julian looked confused at first, but when the furrows on his brow began to flatten out, I couldn't look at him anymore. I covered my eyes with my left hand and swiveled my seated body toward the stairs. The idea of singing in front of people made my hands shake, but I would have rather performed at a packed Carnegie Hall than witness my recorded voice being absorbed by this audience of one.

After Julian stopped playback in the middle of the second verse, I heard him picking up the mouse and putting it down over and over again like a bull pawing the dirt. I turned back toward him when he stopped scrolling and started clicking. At the time, I believed that Julian did what he did next in solidarity, so that I would have company in being embarrassed. Now I think that he probably did it to one-up me, to show that if there was a performer in the room, someone with talent and charisma, it was him. He opened the individual tracks of "Do You Feel Like We Do?" from Peter Frampton's *Frampton Comes Alive!* and put on the headphones. Then he picked up the microphone and held it at his side.

I wheeled over and checked the computer monitor as the

song began. "Julian, you've got Frampton's vocals set to play back in your headset."

"I know," he said.

I figured Julian was using the original vocals as a crutch, either to help him remember the words or hit the right notes. But when the thin black line swept over the image of Frampton's lead vocal, Julian didn't sing. I looked at him, then scrolled through the two-dozen tracks. When I got to the lead-guitar track, I saw what he had in mind. I just didn't believe he could do it.

Julian kept the mike at his side throughout the intro, three verses, four times through the chorus, a short guitar solo and a keyboard solo. Only he could hear the music. I watched it all on the monitor. Then, after six minutes, he began to imitate the sounds of Frampton's most famous guitar solo. A skilled amateur with the right equipment could have played the solo note for note on the guitar. But Julian was playing it with his voice. With each passing second, Julian's blue vocal track mirrored the size, shape and pattern of Frampton's silenced red guitar track, like a string of genetic material being gradually cloned.

For the second movement of his solo, Frampton had employed a talkbox, which compresses the notes from an electric guitar and sends them as vibrations through a piece of plastic tubing taped alongside the lead-vocal microphone. By taking the tubing in his mouth and shaping the sound, Frampton had created the aural illusion that his guitar was singing to the live audience. Julian created the same effect without a talkbox, and without a guitar.

Then Julian dove into the fiery concluding movement, bending the notes through mouth shapes that ranged from the oval to the trapezoidal. His Adam's apple pulled almost out of sight on the high notes and descended into view only when he approached the depths of his range. Another person giving voice to Frampton's notes with a series of "no," "nare," and "wah" sounds might have aped the sort of histrionics that traditionally accompany guitar heroics. But Julian kept his eyes open, his hands on the mike, and his performance free of air guitar.

At the end of the song, Julian tore off the headphones and leaned in toward the monitor. "Let's give it a look," he said.

The discrepancies between Julian's vocals and Frampton's guitar were greater than those between my vocals and Steve Perry's, but smaller than they might have been had Julian played Frampton's solo on an instrument. His precision astounded me.

When we were done analyzing the visuals, Julian got up to leave. I didn't want him to go.

"Wait," I said. "You should do that next week."

Julian looked at me and sat back down. "What?" he asked.

"Sing the guitar part of some song at Whirly Gigs. On Karaoke Monday."

He laughed through his nose, shook his head and stood up again. "I don't think so."

I stood up with him, wobbling a bit. "Think about what a great last stand it would be! A karaoke crowd wouldn't know what to do with a performance like that."

Julian looked at me as if I were losing my mind or, at the very least, too drunk to drive him to the El. I bent over the console, took the mouse in my hand, clicked once, twice, then double clicked. Cued to its final minute, "Do You Feel Like We Do?" erupted through the speakers with Julian's vocal track in place of Frampton's guitar. As accurate as they were, Julian's unmixed notes sounded ridiculous backed by the instruments recorded live at San Francisco's Winterland in 1975. Julian smiled and we both laughed out loud, though our laughter was nearly drowned out by the playback. He put his hand on my shoulder and squeezed, and I wrapped my left arm around his waist and pulled him toward me.

Then the basement door opened.

"Brian?"

Julian and I pulled apart immediately.

"Brian, it's three in the morning," my mother said. "Can you keep it down?"

"All right," I said.

As I turned the volume down, my face flushed. I hadn't called her mom, and she hadn't called me son, but there could have been little doubt in Julian's mind to whom that voice belonged. Her tone and our dynamic said it all. Now I did want Julian to leave, not because of anything he'd said or done, but because he had seen me as I really was.

With my head down, I grabbed my car keys. Julian, getting the message, picked up his keys and wallet from the console and pushed them into the front pockets of his jeans. Then he followed me out the door and to my car.

For the first few miles of the drive to the El station, we were silent.

"It's not a big deal, you know," he said, eventually. "Living with your parents, I mean. A lot of people I know do it. And you've got such a great setup down there! I wouldn't ever want to move—"

"Thanks, but can you just—?" I tried to smile through my shame, but came up short. I did manage to exhale and start over. "Thanks."

The incident with my mother wasn't even my largest source of embarrassment. I could still feel my hand on Julian's belt, grabbing it and pulling him toward me. At the thought of Julian replaying the corresponding sensation in his own head, I wanted to make a deep, exhausted, guttural sound that would have forced my tongue out of my mouth. But I had to swallow that urge for another mile or so.

I rolled to a stop in front of the station stairs, put the car in park, and kept my eyes straight ahead. I was aware that this would probably be the last time I saw Julian, but I didn't want to look at him.

"I'll be over tomorrow," he said. "Around eight. We've only got a week to put this thing together."

It took me a moment to realize that he was talking about performing at Whirly Gigs.

"They're going to hate us," Julian said, smiling. Then he clapped me on the shoulder blade with his left hand, got out of the car, and closed the door behind him.

The next night, we found a song worthy of Julian's talent. Over the next five evenings, we put Julian's rehearsals up against the original lead guitar track of Cream's "White Room," noted each difference, and honed his rendition into a precise sonic imitation.

In spare moments at work, I laid out a graphic treatment to accompany Julian's performance. When I had leaded and kerned the type to my satisfaction and synchronized text to sound, I burned the finished product to a DVD. If Julian's voice-guitar would be the blow to the gut of karaoke nation, I imagined my graphics would dig the knuckles deeper.

On the final night, after rehearsing until almost four in the morning, I asked Julian if he wanted to crash at my place instead of heading home. He declined. I offered to drive him home or to the El. He said he had money for a cab, slapped me on the back, and left.

The following Monday, we walked north from the Belmont station toward Whirly Gigs. When we approached Starmakers, I looked away, as did Julian. But there was no way to avert our ears. A woman half in the bag and half a measure behind the accompaniment was singing Billy Joel's "Only The Good Die Young." She didn't sound young, but she was certainly dying up there.

A few paces after the woman fell out of earshot, I voiced the question that had been on my mind the whole trip up here.

"What are we doing?" I asked.

Julian stopped and squinted at me. "What do you mean?"

"If you go up there and do this tonight, are we any different than that woman in there? Sure, you're doing the guitar, not the vocals, and you're better than she is, but what we're doing is still karaoke—at a karaoke night, on a karaoke stage." I lifted my palms and smiled hysterically. "I might as well get up there and sing 'Faithfully.' Would it be any different?"

Julian nodded, turned, and resumed his march toward Whirly Gigs without saying a word.

"Julian," I said, walking after him. When I put my hand

on his shoulder, he whirled around, knocking it off with a windmill-swing of his right arm. I flinched and gave a shallow, startled gasp. I recognized the look in his eyes, having seen him give it to bands with no talent, women who couldn't dress, and men who wouldn't leave him alone. It was disgust. He took a breath and ran his fingers through his hair, seeming suddenly aware that he was in public.

"Look," he said. "You helped me find my mistakes and fix them, and you did the graphics. But I do the performing. So I guess I don't need you anymore."

He said the words matter-of-factly, with only the barest hint of malice, but they struck a heavy blow, and pulverized the notion that Julian and I were somehow in league together.

When I made no reply, Julian started walking. I let him get a half-block ahead, then followed him. The moment wasn't mine anymore, but I still couldn't bring myself to miss it. Besides, I had nowhere else to go.

I took my usual seat at the bar. Casey arched one eyebrow, poured me a bourbon, and handed it to me without a word. Julian was talking to the karaoke DJ, punctuating the rhythms of his speech with small movements of the DVD case he held in his hand. The DJ nodded his assent to whatever Julian was saying, took the DVD, and went backstage. Julian sat on the stool closest to the stage and turned his back on it.

Julian's regular booth was occupied by two Korean couples, laughing loudly and speaking in their native language. They were surrounded by casualties of what appeared to be a sizable after-work happy hour that had moved north from Downtown. A man from the happy-hour crowd guided an unsteady woman by the elbow to a spot a few feet away from my stool and proposed, in a whisper he probably thought was discreet, that she leave her husband for him. She demurred, citing the man's "sexual problem." I cleared my throat a few times to get them to move away, but they didn't.

To kick off Karaoke Monday at Whirly Gigs, one of the Korean women performed a stunning rendition of Whitney Houston's "The Greatest Love of All" without so much as glancing at the words. The happy-hour crowd ate it up. Then one of their own, a man I had seen standing alongside a booth listening to conversations in which he was never directly addressed, took the stage and sang Kris Kristofferson's "Sunday Morning Coming Down." His rendition was competent but boring, and the Koreans joined his coworkers in ignoring him.

As the man placed the microphone in its stand, the DJ said, "All right. Please welcome Julian to the Karaoke Monday stage. Julian, are you here?"

Julian drained his bourbon, swiveled on his stool, and walked calmly and coolly to the stage. By the time he got up there, the perfunctory applause had extinguished. He pulled the microphone from the stand and stood with his arms at his side.

The screen behind him changed from green to a rich black. In silence, 84-point white Futura type reading "White Room" appeared against the black background for a moment and faded slowly to black. When the first haunting bars of the song rang out, no images appeared on the screen, and as the song's original first-verse vocals played loud and clear over the portable sound system, Julian kept his mouth shut.

We had been sure that this close-mouthed protest would raise the ire of the karaoke fans. But now, as I looked around the room, the Koreans were laughing at a private joke while, over my right shoulder, the unsteady woman was in the midst of another refusal to leave her husband for her lover. This time I actually heard her say "erectile dysfunction."

Eventually, a man with a red necktie loosened beneath his collar cupped his hand around the right side of his mouth and yelled, "Hey buddy! If you're going to lip synch, move your lips!"

I exhaled. Finally, Julian was getting some fraction of the hatred he had hoped for. He seemed to be resisting the urge to smile.

Casey put another bourbon down for me. "What's he doing?" he asked, his eyes on Julian.

"He's about to start," I said.

"Start what?"

"Singing the guitar parts."

Casey turned to me. "Singing the guitar parts?"

The song entered verse two and I realized that, in a few seconds, no explanation would be necessary. After Jack Bruce sang the verse's opening line, Julian flawlessly rendered Eric Clapton's howling, bending notes with his voice. The moment the first sound left his mouth, white text exploded on the black screen: "Bow, wha goo wow ooh wow wow wow owe owe owe own." The combination of text and sound won the Koreans' attention.

After the second line, Julian hit Clapton's notes again: "Whoa ooo-wow-ooo-wow-ooo-wow, ooo wow ah-ooo-whan wow." As I witnessed my bold graphic mockery of karaoke convention, I flushed with pride and excitement. But both pride and excitement cooled when I remembered that Julian had claimed my work—and this moment—for himself alone.

By the end of verse two, the Koreans had returned to their conversation, the happy-hour crowd seemed more bored than annoyed, and Casey had turned his back on the stage to mix a martini. Even the DJ had his head down, cueing up the next song. I was the only one watching Julian now. We might as well have been in my parents' basement.

As verse three began, Julian seemed to notice the crowd's indifference. He began pounding his heel in rhythm with the drums. His diaphragm clenched visibly beneath his tight black t-shirt, and his mouth and throat performed the complicated contortions required to imitate the open-door-closed-door effect of the wah-wah pedal. Hitting even the high notes cleanly, he screeched and squealed and roared with confidence.

And still they ignored him.

When the final solo began, Julian slammed the mike into its stand. He braced his right wrist against his pelvic bone, pinned his left elbow against his ribs, and held his left hand in the air with its back to the audience. Julian recreated the sound of Clapton's solo with staggering fidelity, capturing the energy and emotion of the playing in his voice. All the while, he picked and fingered an imaginary guitar.

Feeling sick to my stomach, I put my elbow on the bar and shielded my eyes with my hand.

"Is this part of the act?" Casey asked.

I didn't answer. Finally, mercifully, the song faded out and Julian returned his arms to his side.

"Let's hear it for Julian," the DJ said.

The audience offered a few whoops and a short round of applause. Julian walked off the stage with his hands in his pockets and his head down. I slid off my stool and walked out to the main floor to meet him. He passed me without so much as a glance. I stood there facing the stage, feeling exposed on all sides. I touched my jeans to assure myself I wasn't naked and headed back to the receding comforts of my stool.

Having sung a guitar solo, played the air guitar and pandered to an audience he knew to be beneath him, Julian would never allow himself to return to Whirly Gigs. The performance had been a clean break with the club, and a clean break with me. Whatever we had been must have mattered to Julian at least as much as Whirly Gigs had; he'd put the torch to both. And I had helped him gather the tinder.

"All right," the DJ said. "Let's get our next performer up here. Give it up for Tommy, everybody."

Tommy, the alleged sufferer of erectile dysfunction, staggered to the front of the stage. The top three buttons of his oxford shirt had come undone, revealing a v-neck undershirt and a thin patch of long, scraggly black hairs. "This is for you, Lisa," he yelled, causing the speakers to screech earsplitting feedback. Then, his brow furrowed in earnest emotion, Tommy began to sing over the backing track of "Love Will Keep Us Together." He was sharp on every note. Lisa, clearly mortified, put her drink on a table and hurried to the ladies' room. Some of her and Tommy's colleagues laughed at the spectacle, while others put their heads down or covered their eyes. But I kept my eyes on Tommy, and applauded politely when he finished. Then I got Casey's attention, pointed at my credit card by the register, and pointed at the stage. Tommy's next drink was on me, and his song choice was only part of my reason for buying it.

While one of the Koreans performed Human League's "Don't You Want Me," I sat on my stool, sipped my bourbon, and listened. Karaoke, it turned out, presented some interesting audio conundrums, like the variable volume levels of the backing tracks, and a performer's struggle to determine the appropriate distance between his mouth and the microphone. They were sonic images simple enough for me to envision on my own, without Julian, and whether the hipsters would have admitted it or not, these performers were no worse than some of the bands we had seen over the years.

And as I sat on foam padding compressed into a mold of my buttocks, I decided I wanted a clean break, too—from the old Whirly Gigs, and from the absence pulsing from the empty stool beside me. I looked around at the Koreans, and at Tommy leaning over the drink I had bought him, and realized that I could make my clean break right where Julian had made his, and that I could do it my way, without torching anything or hurting anyone. My path was laid out straight: four minutes of hot pink peaks, valleys and flatlands magnified one-hundred times.

At the thought of taking the stage, I started to sweat, and saliva thickened in my throat. Keep your eyes closed, I told myself, and all you'll see is sound.

I wiped my forehead with my hand and scanned the tables for a thick black binder. I spotted it in a booth occupied by Lisa, whose chin was bobbing with half-sleep, and two of her female coworkers. With the club's north wall, the two ladies formed a perimeter around Lisa, probably to protect her from Tommy's drunken advances. As I approached, the guards stiffened.

"Excuse me," I said, pointing at the binder on the table. "Can I borrow that?"

"Suit yourself," the woman next to Lisa said.

I picked up the binder and a stubby half-pencil and brought them to a table near the stage. I flipped to the Fs, found "Faithfully," and jotted its alphanumeric code on a white slip of paper. Then I mounted the stage, handed the paper to the DJ, and waited my turn in the wings.

THINGLESS

Kyle woke up to a terrifying realization: he would start high school in two weeks and he had yet to find a thing. He hadn't had a thing in junior high, and that had worked out okay, but El Dorado High had almost thirteen-hundred students. Kyle was sure that if he showed up on the first day of high school without a thing, he'd be swept up in the swarm and lost for good.

He'd seen it happen. Two years ago, Kyle's next-door neighbor, Starlee, had started high school knowing exactly what her thing would be. She'd been co-captain of the dance team in junior high and spent three years choreographing, rehearsing and performing routines. Watching her lithe, precise movements during the halftime shows of junior-high football games, Kyle had marveled that Starlee, who'd begun to get her body, was the same girl with whom he'd spent so many summer nights playing Ghosts in the Graveyard. Back then, Kyle had considered himself Starlee's equal—her better where running and choosing hiding places were concerned—but by junior high, running and hiding weren't the yardsticks anymore. The year Kyle was in sixth grade and Starlee was in eighth, they spent every day at the same small school, and evenings and weekends in homes just fifteen feet apart, but they rarely said a word to one another.

Two weeks after enrolling at El Dorado High, Starlee was cut from the dance team. After that, she stopped doing her hair and putting on makeup. She was home from school by three-thirty most every day and emerged from the house only to smoke cigarettes on the crumbling slab of concrete at her back door. Kyle could not remember the last time he saw Starlee smile. If not having a thing could bring a creature like Starlee so low, Kyle shuddered to think what thinglessness would do to him.

Kyle had supposed that his thing—the thing he was meant to have—would manifest itself somehow, perhaps as a hand-me-down from an older cousin or a gleam in the mud of a creek bank. Such a revelation was still possible, Kyle figured, but he could no longer afford to wait for it.

For some time, Kyle had thought that the guitar would make a good thing. He liked the look of a guitar, the bowed symmetry of the body and the slight angle at which the head emerged from the neck. Guitars looked cool in a way that Kyle didn't. But more importantly, guys who made the guitar their thing put themselves outside the usual pecking order. They didn't sit around wishing they'd made the football team or been elected to student government. They hung out in each other's backyards and carports, playing and singing. Kyle knew he wasn't going to top the pecking order at El Dorado High, and he didn't think he would want to if he could, so getting outside it seemed like good idea.

With time running short, Kyle didn't bother to consider

other options. He dressed without showering and walked a mile and a half in the South Arkansas heat to the music store near the community college, carrying all of his graduation and lawn-mowing money—150 dollars—in the right hip pocket of his shorts.

When Kyle pushed open the store's front door, rusted bells rang above him and a sweet-and-sour combination of resin and cigarette smoke filled his nose. An older man sat on a stool behind the glass case that served as the store's counter. He smoked a cigarette. On the pegboard walls to his left and right and behind him, dozens of guitars hung vertically from rubber-coated brackets.

"I'd like to get a guitar," Kyle said to the older man.

"OK," the man said. He did not get up from the stool.

"What kind of guitar should I get?" Kyle asked.

"That depends. How much money do you have to spend?"

"A hundred and fifty."

The man extinguished his cigarette and slid gingerly from the stool. He sidestepped out from behind the glass case and walked toward the wall to his right. Kyle eyed the guitars in the man's path. Would he pull down the black one with the mother-of-pearl inlays? Or the one with the Mexican drawings on the front? Near the front door, the man reached up for a standard spruce-top model and lifted it gently from its bracket. He held the guitar's body to his chin, closed one eye, and looked down the neck as if checking a rifle sight. Then he handed the guitar to Kyle, who leaned away a little when he took the instrument, afraid that he might hit himself in the mouth with it somehow.

"What kind is it?" Kyle asked.

"A Dean."

On the Internet, Kyle had been reading about Gibsons and Martins and Taylors. "Are Deans good?"

"They're good for the money," the man said. "This model's worth two-fifty, but it's on sale for one-thirty-five. That sale price means no returns, so you'll have to be sure you want it."

Kyle looked the instrument over, turning it awkwardly and feeling its weight in his hands. "I want it."

"You sure?" the man said.

Kyle nodded. He handed the guitar to the man, pulled a wad of bills from his shorts, and set it on the counter.

After giving Kyle his change and a receipt, the man sat down on his stool and tuned the guitar one string at a time. Then he began making shapes on the fingerboard with his left hand and strumming them into sound with his right thumb. Kyle wanted to be able to make one of those shapes, but the man didn't hold any one of them long enough for Kyle to memorize it.

"You know any chords?" the man asked.

Kyle wasn't sure what a chord was. He shook his head.

"You want to be a rocker?"

"Sure."

"I'll teach you a good rock chord. Once you know this one you can play a half-dozen others." The man flattened his left index finger against all six strings at the first fret, then placed the callused tip of his middle finger on a string at the second fret and his ring and pinky fingertips on separate strings at the third. Then he ran his thumb down the strings over the sound hole.

"Which chord is that?"

"F," the man said.

Kyle liked the sound of F.

"You try." The man stood up and offered the guitar to Kyle. When Kyle had the guitar body secured between his elbow and his side, the man pulled Kyle's left index finger straight and mashed it against the strings at the first fret. Then he placed three of Kyle's fingertips on the strings, digging the phosphor bronze into the soft pink skin. Kyle began strumming while the man's fingers were still on his.

"Hold on a minute, now," the man said. Then he took two steps back. "Now try."

Kyle pulled his thumb down over the strings. His F didn't sound like the man's. He felt the fourth string vibrating beneath the tip of his pinky and pressed it harder, but the center knuckle buckled and muted several strings, so he stopped.

"There you go," the man said.

The man threw in a black chipboard case for free, so Kyle walked out of the store with a guitar, a case, ten white plastic picks and four dollars. As he carried home his soon-to-be-thing, Kyle bounced on the balls of his feet just a little and clenched his jaw to keep himself from smiling.

Until that summer, Kyle had thought that Starlee didn't have any friends. But since July, two guys who looked a little older than her and a lot older than Kyle had been pulling up in front of Starlee's house every day around lunchtime in an older-model Camaro. Starlee would let them in and almost immediately turn up her music—all fuzz and feedback and whiny singing, not the dance music she'd listened to in junior high. Kyle could hear it clearly through the open double-hung window in his parents' room, where he whiled away summer days on his father's computer. The guys were always gone before Starlee's mother got home from work. When they left, the music would stop, and Kyle could hear the crows cawing in the tall pines down the block.

The day after getting the guitar, Kyle spent the afternoon on the edge of his parents' bed strumming F chord after F chord. Most sounded better than the one he'd played in the store, though none rang as clearly as the one the man had played. When the fingertips of his left hand began to burn, Kyle would blow on them and examine the dents he'd pressed into them with the strings. Starlee's music blared out her open windows, but it registered with Kyle as white noise, like a box fan or a dryer running. All he heard was the F chord the man had played at the store. When the burning had subsided, Kyle would lay his index finger over the first fret, fit the strings back into the grooves in his fingertips, and try again to make the sound he heard in his head.

Around four, the rumble of the Camaro accelerating down the block swamped Kyle's F chords. As the rumble faded, Starlee's music cut off abruptly. Through his parents' bedroom window, Kyle saw Starlee step onto her back step and light up a cigarette. An oversized white t-shirt nearly concealed her short red nylon shorts. Both the base and the tips of her ponytail were gathered high on the back of her head with a single rubber band.

Kyle could only play one chord—hardly enough to have made the guitar his thing—but he felt quite a bit different than he had just a few days ago. He wondered if anyone else could see the change in him. He wondered if Starlee could see it.

He laid the guitar down gently on his parents' bed and scampered down the hall, stopping to gather himself before opening the screen door. Then he stepped out onto the rotting wood porch, hopped down from the top step, and walked with his hands in his pockets to the fence that divided the fifteen feet of gravel, dirt, and patchy crabgrass between his house and Starlee's. Starlee blew smoke up and away, as if aiming for the tall pines. Her screen door was closed, but the thick white door behind it was open.

"Hey, Starlee."

She finished exhaling her smoke and glanced at him. "Hey, Kyle."

The up-and-down lilt that Kyle remembered in Starlee's voice had flattened out. What remained of it sounded like an accident of muscle memory, or a put-on.

"How you been?" Kyle asked.

"All right," she said.

"Good." Kyle tried to keep his eyes off of Starlee's long legs and was almost grateful that her t-shirt shrouded the rest of her shape. For her part, Starlee seemed to be staring into the thick mess of vines and scrub trees that made the back boundary of her mother's lot all but impassable. He and Starlee hadn't had a conversation this long in years, so Kyle didn't waste any more time on small talk. "What kind of music do you listen to?" he asked.

She shrugged. "All kinds of stuff."

"What kind of music were you listening to today?"

Starlee glanced at Kyle a second time. She nibbled at a cuticle, then examined it while the cigarette burned slowly in her other hand. "Neutral Milk Hotel," she said.

"Oh," Kyle said.

"Have you heard them?" she asked.

"No," he said. "Well, I've never heard them and known it was them." Kyle smiled. "Maybe I should listen a little closer to what's coming out your windows."

Then Starlee looked squarely at Kyle. She tossed her cigarette on the gravel driveway, opened the screen door, and pushed past the white door with a long, purposeful stride. Before Kyle could figure out what he'd done wrong, Starlee reemerged from the house, walked to the fence, and held a CD over Kyle's side of the property line. "You can have this," she said.

She'd gripped the disc in the creases on the undersides of her first knuckles, and Kyle grabbed it the same way, momentarily interlacing his fingers with hers but never touching them. The bottom side of the disc shone purple and green in the sunlight. On the title side, "Neutral Milk Hotel" had been scrawled in green laundry marker above the spindle hole. "On Avery Island" was written below it in the same hand.

"Don't be listening to anything going on in my house," Starlee said. She stared at Kyle, as if waiting for him to acknowledge the order.

"OK," Kyle said. He knew he could manage not to listen, but he wondered how he'd keep from hearing anything with both houses' windows open and Starlee playing her music so loud.

Starlee went back inside her house. The screen door slapped twice against the wooden frame, and the thick white door closed behind it.

Kyle went into his parents' bedroom, put the Neutral Milk Hotel CD into his father's computer and clicked the on-screen play button. The songs sounded like mistakes at first—recordings that should have been thrown away and done over—but after hearing the first few tracks Kyle figured out that the fuzzy songs were supposed to sound fuzzy, and the clear songs were supposed to sound clear. Fuzzy or clear, each song seemed sad if Kyle listened to the words, so eventually he ignored them and absorbed only the music: chords strummed on a guitar that didn't sound much better than Kyle's own, and melodies carried by organs, horns and the raw, vibratoless voice of the singer.

The music evoked feelings of otherness in Kyle: this isn't for me, he thought, by which he meant that he was neither as cool nor as weird as he perceived the music to be. But he kept listening, and as he listened he thought about Starlee. When the album ended, Kyle could not have told you for certain whether Starlee seemed melancholy because of her music or the music seemed melancholy because of Starlee.

Though he'd listened to twelve songs, Kyle found, in the near-silence of his parents' bedroom, that he couldn't shake the beat and melody of the album's first song. He hummed some semblance of the tune and kept time slapping his thigh. Then he listened to the song again. The lyrics—about pornography and drugs and fires—scared Kyle a little. He couldn't tell what was a joke and what was deadly serious.

Kyle googled a phrase from the lyrics, hoping he might understand them better if he could read them. The first page of search results all pointed to a song called "Song Against Sex." Kyle didn't recall hearing those words sung together and, though it was partly about sex, the song didn't seem to be *against* sex, exactly. Kyle clicked on the second search result. "Song Against Sex" was indeed the song roaring out of his father's computer speakers. On screen, the words were easier to comprehend and even more unsettling.

The letter F and a word Kyle had never seen before—"Bbmaj"—were written above each line of the lyrics. Kyle scrolled up to the top of the page and realized that these were the song's chords: F and B flat major. He could hardly believe that a song this full could be made with only two chords, one of which was the only chord he could play. The page included two crude, typographic diagrams—x characters on a lattice of underlines and vertical bars—that showed how to form each of the song's chords on a fingerboard. Kyle copied the B-flat-major diagram into a new document and printed it. Then, with "Song Against Sex" still coursing through his head, Kyle took the guitar in his hands.

For the next week and a half, Kyle spent at least a few hours a day in the den, a small, dark room at the corner of the house farthest from Starlee's back step. First, he worked on his transition from the F chord to the B flat major right below it. Getting his fingers into the right shape from a resting position was one thing; going from F to B flat major and back again proved quite another. To play "Song Against Sex," Kyle had to slow the song to a fitful crawl. He hardly recognized it.

When he could execute each chord change in a second or two, Kyle started singing the song as he played it. After a few days, he had the lyrics memorized. He was still singing and playing the up-tempo rocker at the pace of a country ballad, but he was playing it through without any stops and starts. And when his voice strained to reach a high note or his fingers touched strings they shouldn't have, Kyle's version of "Song Against Sex" captured some of the rawness of the original, and he felt something surge inside him.

After ten days, Kyle knew he had "Song Against Sex" down well enough to play along with the recording. But the family's only CD player was in his father's computer, within earshot—and eyeshot—of Starlee's back step. That fact made him hesitate, but Kyle decided he'd worked too hard not to hear his guitar backed by the drums, bass, vocals, and trombone of Neutral Milk Hotel, and that, when he got down to it, he wanted Starlee to hear him play. So he sat on his parents' bed, waiting for those guys to leave Starlee's house and for her music to stop. The boldness of it all excited Kyle. What are you doing, man? he asked himself, smiling. There were reasons not to make such a bald attempt to impress Starlee, and Kyle was aware of them, but he convinced himself that school's beginning—just three days away—offered a kind of clean slate. With bells and homework and rumors and football games, would Starlee even remember whether or not he'd played? Would Kyle?

Kyle wondered who had made the music that filled the air between Starlee's house and his own today. He was pretty sure it wasn't Neutral Milk Hotel. I'll ask her later, Kyle thought. But then he remembered that Starlee had told him not to listen to anything going on in her house, and asking would mean admitting he'd been listening. Before Kyle could lift a phrase from the lyrics and search for it, the music stopped. A minute later, the Camaro started up and rumbled away.

Kyle sat motionless on the bed, breathing through his mouth, waiting for what would come next. He heard Starlee's back door squeeze out of its heat-swollen frame and the screen door creak on its hinges. Her bare leg hit the concrete first and the rest of her followed. She was wearing red shorts and a gray t-shirt one size too small. She lit a cigarette, and when she'd exhaled her first deep drag, Kyle pushed himself to his feet and turned up the volume on his father's computer speakers. Then he grabbed his guitar, sat down on the rolling desk chair, and rested the guitar on his thigh. As he moved the cursor to the play button with his right hand, he made the shape of an F chord with his left.

During the ten seconds of feedback and chatter at the beginning of the recording, Kyle took his white Fender pick in hand and held it above the sound hole. The drummer clicked off the rhythm with his sticks, and the guitarist began to play. And when the singer came in four bars later, Kyle played his own guitar, spreading a layer of clear acoustic tones above the fuzz of the recording. He stared hard at the fingerboard, making sure to hit only the strings he was supposed to this time. He wanted Starlee to hear he could play.

After verse one, Kyle wondered if she could hear him at all. He'd set the volume loud enough to get her attention, but was the recording drowning him out? What if she thought he was simply blasting her own music back at her through his father's computer speakers? What would she make of that?

Kyle looked out the window and found Starlee leaning her shoulder against the back of her house and facing his own. Then he mangled an F and returned his eyes to the fingerboard until he was back in sync with the song. When he looked up again, Starlee was staring at the ground between their houses. Her forelock hung in front of her face, keeping Kyle from getting a look at her eyes. She wasn't smoking anymore. She was just standing on her back step, listening.

As the final verse began, Kyle's stomach flooded with emotion and he strummed so hard he worried a string might break and blind him. "Song Against Sex" built to its climax—the speaker's threat to light himself on fire—and Kyle played loud and hard and clean until the song petered out with three lazy descending notes from the trombone.

When he looked up, Starlee was gone.

Kyle leaned his guitar against the desk and wiped his sweaty face with the front of his t-shirt. Now he was the kind of kid who taught himself strange songs and slyly serenaded older girls. Maybe he always had been but hadn't known it. Maybe his thing made him who he really was.

Kyle spent the following morning playing B flat major and F chords without any rhythm or purpose. He glanced out the window every few minutes, hoping Starlee would come out of her house to smoke or cool off or take out the garbage. He was sure that she would see him differently now and wanted to feel her eyes on him.

By that afternoon, Kyle still hadn't been seen by Starlee, and he feared that whatever good his performance had done him was waning. To take the edge off his impatience, Kyle carried his guitar to the den, leaned it against the arm of the yarn-upholstered couch, and turned on the television. Every few minutes, he muted the sound, hoping to find that Starlee's music had stopped. At four-thirty, it was still blaring. What can be taking so long? Kyle wondered.

Too antsy to sit any longer, Kyle walked out the back door and around to the front yard. The Camaro was still parked in front of Starlee's house. It was painted in a matte-finish black, and two hubcaps were missing. All the driver's money must be going into the rumble, Kyle thought. That must be his thing.

Suddenly Starlee's music cut off right in the middle of a song, and her front door opened. Her two usual guests stepped out. The bigger one—they were both big—closed the door behind him. Kyle watched them as they walked toward the Camaro. When they noticed him and stopped, Kyle shifted his gaze to the house across the street.

"What are you looking at, boy?" the smaller one asked.

"Nothing," Kyle said. He'd never noticed that the house across the street was peach-colored until now. He'd always thought it was yellow.

"Show's over," the bigger one said. He lowered the curved brim of his ball cap over his eyes and pulled a ring of keys from the left hip pocket of his jeans. "Run along now."

Kyle didn't say anything, but he didn't move either. He didn't want to run along. He was in his own yard.

The bigger one took a step toward him. "Did you hear me, boy?"

Kyle knew the two guys would have no qualms about leaping the chain-link fence and giving him hell, so he walked toward his backyard, but slowly. The bigger one said something under his breath and the smaller one laughed. Then the engine started up, and the Camaro rumbled away.

When Kyle reached the backyard, Starlee was standing at the fence holding an unlit cigarette in her hands. Kyle felt himself get scared, more scared than he'd been of her friends.

"What are you doing talking to them?"

Her tone made him wince. "I wasn't. They were talking to me."

"What were you doing so close to my house?"

"Nothing." Had he been that close to her house? "I was just walking around 'cause I was bored."

Starlee shook her head and smiled bitterly. "Well," she said, "I bet you're not bored anymore." Then she stalked off, throwing open the screen door and disappearing inside her house. The thick back door thudded shut, rattling her kitchen windows.

Kyle could feel the humid air between his lips as he stared at the spot where Starlee had just been standing. He replayed the confrontation in his head, trying to figure out what he'd done. He'd been threatened and scolded in the space of two minutes and, so far as Kyle could tell, standing in his own yard had been his only offense.

He retreated to the den and lay down on the couch. Every chord he'd strummed to show Starlee how he'd changed sawed at his insides like a jagged blade. Maybe she would forget everything he'd done when school started, but Kyle knew he never would.

After a few minutes, Kyle rolled onto his feet. He wrapped his hands around the neck of the guitar and picked it up. Then he swung it slowly in front of his waist like a batter waiting for a pitcher to get a sign he liked. He imagined how it would feel to bring the body down on the arm of the couch, driving through until whatever was left in his hands had hit the floor. He wondered how many swings it would take to shatter the body like an eggshell.

Kyle sat down on the couch and rested the guitar's curve

on his right thigh. He strummed an F chord, then a B flat major. Then he started to play "Song Against Sex" at full speed, without any accompaniment. He sang, too, filling lines he couldn't recall with words from other verses. He had to try like hell to remember the lyrics and keep the rhythm and make the right shapes with his hand, but through it all, Kyle realized that playing the guitar felt different than it had the day before. He was playing—at least in part—because of what had just happened with Starlee. But he wasn't playing for her. He wasn't playing for anyone else, either. He was just playing. Playing was just what he did. The realization buoyed Kyle somehow, and the buoyancy came through in his playing. He stomped his left foot on the carpet with each beat and strummed as hard as he could without losing all control. Even his head swiveled with the rhythm. And as he sang the melody of the trombone solo over the jangle of his messy chords, Kyle thought, *This* is what it feels like to have a thing. This must be.

Around noon, Kyle sat down at his father's computer, determined to learn at least part of another song before school started the next day. He maxed out the speakers' volume to drown out Starlee's music and listened to the Neutral Milk Hotel album two times through with the guitar by his side, waiting for something to hit him the way "Song Against Sex" had. Nothing did. So Kyle picked a song that sounded simple. By Kyle's count, the slow, plaintive, "Someone is Waiting" had only three chords. A tablature site confirmed the number of chords and named them: F, B flat major, and C. Kyle couldn't believe his luck. Though he likely could play dozens of chords, the guitarist for Neutral Milk Hotel was partial, it seemed, to the two Kyle knew already.

The song's tablature included diagrams for open C and barred C, which was just B flat major played two frets further up the fingerboard. But from the moment he realized that a C chord could be played without flattening a finger against a fret and bending his wrist around the guitar neck, Kyle focused only on open C. Following the diagram, he placed the tips of his index, middle and ring fingers on the strings. The shape felt natural, almost ergonomic. Kyle's choice was rewarded again when he dragged the pick across the strings. The open C rang out in a way that even a perfectly executed barred chord, with so much flesh on the strings, could not. Kyle hadn't known his guitar could sound that good. He played open C after open C. With each strum, the strings wobbled wildly, settled into a tight blur, and came to rest as the chord faded into Starlee's music.

When he had the C down, Kyle played an F, a B flat major, and an open C in succession. Getting his fingers in the right places and sounding each chord once took almost half a minute. "Someone is Waiting" was a slow song, but not nearly slow enough for Kyle to play it—not today, anyway.

As Kyle sat in the rolling chair, struggling with the chord progression, a melody from Starlee's house pierced his concentration. Starlee was listening to "Someone is Waiting." Had she heard him listening to the song? Had she heard him butchering Fs and Cs and B flat majors? Was she sending him some kind of message? An apology, maybe?

Kyle stood up and traced the music's path with his eyes through a dirty steel screen that made everything inside Starlee's living room look pixilated and gray, like images read from a pirated videotape. Kyle saw those two guys kneeling on the carpeted floor, facing each other with their jeans bunched around their calves. Starlee was on her hands and knees, moving—or being moved—back and forth between them. The guys were smiling at each other, as if Starlee weren't even there.

It took Kyle a few seconds to understand what he was seeing. Then he turned and stood with his back to the window, feeling his heartbeat in his ears. Even with his back turned, his parents' bedroom seemed too close to it all. He closed the window, keeping his eyes on his bare feet. Then he walked to the den, sat on the couch, and gripped the sweaty hair above his temples.

But sitting in the den didn't reduce Kyle's sense of alarm. I should be doing something, Kyle thought. But what? Ringing her doorbell? Making a ruckus? Starting a fire? It occurred to Kyle that what he should be doing—what other guys he knew would be doing—was watching through the window, imagining themselves in place of one of those guys, or both of them. But Kyle didn't want to. It occurred to Kyle that not wanting to watch might make him queer, but he didn't see that there was anything he could do about that right now.

Eventually the Camaro rumbled away, and Kyle knew it was over. But he stayed in the den until it was time for dinner, ate with his back to Starlee's house, and went straight to bed. He didn't want to see Starlee on her back step, confirming with her calm, smoky exhalations that what had happened today—or something like it—had happened many times before.

Kyle lay awake, helplessly generating more questions. Did Starlee like doing what he'd seen her doing? Did she love one of those guys, or both of them? Did everyone at school know about this? If they didn't, Kyle figured they would by tomorrow afternoon. Those guys wouldn't see any reason to keep their mouths shut and, if high school was anything like junior high, word would spread in a hurry. Part of Kyle couldn't even blame those guys for blabbing. If he had done what they'd done today, wouldn't he have felt compelled to tell someone? But the thought that this was what kids at school would think of when they saw Starlee—that this was, in effect, her thing—made Kyle roll over on his side and groan.

Kyle hated those guys. He hated them for coming into his neighborhood every day with their pointlessly loud engine, and for smiling at one another while Starlee rocked between them. He wished now that he'd stood his ground when they sent him out of his own front yard. "Show's over," the bigger one had said. "Run along now."

At least I didn't run, Kyle thought.

Run along now.

Show's over.

As Kyle connected the taunts he'd absorbed yesterday with the scene he'd witnessed today, his stomach dropped. He sat up and wrapped his arms around his gut, envisioning with searing clarity what would become of him. He'd be fine until the first time those guys saw him in the halls of El Dorado High. They'd shout to get his attention, but Kyle would keep walking. Then they'd explain to their onlooker buddies that he was the kid who'd watched them go at it with Starlee: the little pervert. Kyle would never get the chance to make the guitar his thing. Pervert would stick.

Kyle replayed the confrontation with those guys, hoping for some hint that he was taking their words the wrong way, but he only confirmed his new understanding. Then he played out the memory of his slow retreat to the backyard and felt, in a way he had not in that moment, the fury radiating from Starlee's eyes as she stood at the fence, waiting to demand an accounting.

I bet you're not bored anymore, she'd said.

"Oh no," Kyle whispered. He had not yet considered whether or not Starlee would believe, once word reached her, that he was a pervert. Now he was certain that she believed as much already. The prospect of being ruined at school and in Starlee's eyes for something he hadn't done—at least, not on purpose, and not when they thought he'd done it—was more than Kyle could bear. He threw himself back onto his pillow and curled into a tight fetal ball, trying to squeeze the shame and anxiety out of his stomach.

After a minute, Kyle unclenched and lay there, blinking sweat out of his eyes in the dark. He needed to do something. He might have played his guitar if not for fear of waking up his parents, but even so, Kyle knew that playing the guitar wouldn't fix anything. He needed more than something to do. He needed something that would do some good, a grand gesture that would prove he hadn't been peeping. He couldn't stop those guys from telling people he was a pervert, but he might still convince Starlee that he wasn't what she thought he was.

Kyle got out of bed, pulled a sheet of paper off the pad on his desk, and wrote:

Starlee,

Thanks for the CD. I can play one song off of it now and I'm learning another. The one I know already is pretty easy. If you want, I can come over after school and teach it to you. Let me know.

Kyle

Kyle held the note in his hand and read it over. No one gets caught peeping and then invites himself over to give a guitar lesson, he thought. Starlee would have to see that things didn't add up: her accusation had not been understood because the deed had not been done. And once she understood that, Kyle believed that he and Starlee would be on firm ground. Word would spread about each of them, but they'd have each other and they'd have the guitar. That the guitar was Kyle's thing—in his own mind, anyway—somehow made what people thought of him seem a little less important. Maybe the guitar had enough in it to do the same for Starlee.

With something to do that stood a chance of changing things, Kyle brightened a bit. But as a grand gesture, delivering the note fell short. He wanted Starlee to feel how he felt when he held the guitar in his hands. He wanted her to start thinking of the guitar when she thought of herself.

Kyle looked out his bedroom window. The deep blue sky was clear all the way to the tops of the tall pines down the block. The weather would hold, Kyle figured, and with Starlee leaving for school in just a few hours, the humidity wouldn't have time to do much damage. At the bottom of the note, Kyle scrawled, "P.S. Please bring the guitar inside before you go to school." Then he taped the paper's horizontal edges to the rounded head of the guitar case.

As he eased the screen door closed with his free hand and stepped into the saturated night air, Kyle's first thought was one he hadn't considered: that Starlee or her mother would catch him making his delivery and accuse him of peeping. Kyle stood on the top step of his back porch, listening to the night bugs and weighing the options. Nobody peeps with a guitar, he thought. If I get caught I'll be accused of serenading, which is weird, but not as bad as peeping. But Kyle knew that Starlee was not likely to give him the benefit of the doubt whether he was carrying the guitar or not, and that his father would be furious to learn he'd been out at night for any purpose. The only solution, Kyle decided, was not to get caught.

He crossed the backyard on the balls of his bare feet, lifted the guitar case over the fence and leaned it against a rusting post. Then he hoisted himself up and swung his legs over, making as little contact with the fence as possible. As the chain links settled back into silence, Kyle squatted behind the guitar case, listening for any signs of stirring through the open windows of Starlee's house and his own. Nothing. He took the case in hand and crossed the driveway, stepping gingerly from weed patch to weed patch. Without ever setting foot on Starlee's back step, Kyle leaned the case against the frame of the screen door, leaving the note he'd written facing up and out.

Climbing back over to his side of the fence, Kyle caught the panel of chain links with his feet. The woven snippets of steel rattled against the hollow steel posts as Kyle dismounted and ran inside, closing the back door behind him. He stood in the dark kitchen and listened, half-expecting to hear the Camaro's rumble. But only the hum of the old refrigerator and the muffled buzz of the night bugs reached his ears.

When Kyle got up the next morning, the lights in Starlee's house were on, and the guitar case was still on the back step. He took a shower, toweled off and put on a pair of jeans, wondering all the while how Starlee would react when she saw the guitar case and the note. Would she consider them exhibits A and B, hard evidence that he'd been on her back step at night and violated her space again? Or would she see the gesture as an overwrought apology and, thus, an admission of guilt? Pulling a red t-shirt over his head and putting his arms through the sleeves, Kyle reminded himself that his gesture could very well have the effect he had intended it to have. But when he tried to imagine Starlee reading the note and smiling, even a little, he could not.

Kyle stood in front of the bathroom sink and looked in the mirror. He had always parted his wet hair on the left, allowing it to dry and fluff up a bit as the morning wore on. But today he decided to leave it the way it was, mussed into clumps and runaway strands by the towel drying he'd given it. His thing was the guitar; parted hair didn't seem right. Kyle wondered how the guy who played guitar for Neutral Milk Hotel had worn his hair in high school.

As Kyle stared at his reflection, the Camaro rumbled past his house. Kyle's stomach clenched. They're giving her a ride, he thought. They're bringing her to school to prove the stories they're telling are true.

Kyle headed for the back door in case Starlee had left without seeing the guitar. Leaving it out overnight was one thing. Baking it in the late-August sun was another.

Kyle stepped onto his back porch and stopped. Shards of wood were strewn on either side of the fence that separated his yard from Starlee's. Some of the jagged triangles lay lacquered side up. Others revealed the color and grain of the untreated spruce that Kyle had only glimpsed through the sound hole. The neck lay face up in one piece—it must have broken away cleanly from the heel. Six steel strings fanned out from their chrome tuners. The thinnest string, arcing shallowly from the guitar head to the sparse gravel, shone in the light of the sun.

Kyle imagined one of those guys—the smaller one—coming around back to fetch Starlee, reading the note, and demolishing the guitar before Starlee had seen it or the note. Or maybe she'd watched without the will to stop him. It didn't matter much now.

Kyle left the shards where they were and started walking. The first bell would ring in ten minutes. His thing was gone, and chances were good that by the end of the day he'd have a new thing he didn't want and wouldn't be able to shake.

As he reached the end of the block, Kyle envisioned a scene that made him want to collapse into the crabgrass: Starlee hears the rumble and walks out the back door. She finds Kyle's gift to them both. She takes it in her hands and destroys it. Then she crawls into the back seat of the Camaro and acts as if everything were as it should be.

CAPTIVE AUDIENCE

In the old days, I would listen to almost any stand-up record that came out. That all changed in the late 1980s. By then, the best of the battle-tested veterans had left stand-up for sitcoms, replaced by marketers and middle managers who bunched up the sleeves of their sport coats, played with their hair and did nothing more than tell jokes. And they *made* it! That's what I couldn't believe! These frauds became the faces of stand-up!

No one seemed to notice that the new guard wasn't doing what made the great ones great. The great ones didn't tell jokes. The great ones created characters and told stories. You thought you knew the real Richard Pryor because you'd seen his act? Guess again. That wasn't Richard Pryor up there. That was Richard Pryor the character, conversing with his grandmother and the neighborhood pimp. Haven't you ever wondered how he came up with two hours of jokes to tell? No one has two hours of jokes to tell. Pryor told two hours of *stories*.

By the early 1990s, character and story were dead in stand-up. Jokes reigned, and I blamed television. So one day,

I pushed my TV, a cathode-ray tube built into an enormous oak cabinet, out the door of my apartment and dragged my recliner closer to my grandmother's record player, a carved-cherry relic of the days when a stereo's performance was less important than its serving, in a pinch, as a buffet table. When I had found the spot in which the words from the built-in speaker hit my ear with the utmost potency, I nailed the recliner to the floor.

From the day I threw out my television—June 4, 1992—I structured my life around the records of the masters: Pryor, Robert Klein, Lily Tomlin, Jonathan Winters, a few others. Eventually, I developed a rotation of fifty-seven albums. Each master's works were interspersed chronologically throughout, allowing me to maintain a sense of each comedian's development while avoiding overexposure to any one voice. For example, Jonathan Winters' debut album, *The Wonderful World of Jonathan Winters*, held the number four spot in the rotation. His follow-up effort, *Down to Earth*, was sixteenth, and *Whistle Stopping with Jonathan Winters* was number fifty-six. Listening from mid-morning to late evening, it took five days for me to hear all fifty-seven albums. When the needle lifted from the final side of the final record, I savored a sense of accomplishment in silence. I was little more than a receptor of genius but, in my appreciation, I was nothing short of virtuosic.

After nine months of the fifty-seven-album rotation—the Heinz Cycle, as I'd come to call it—the unthinkable happened. *Whistle Stopping with Jonathan Winters* concluded with a thud. I wasn't laughing. I wasn't even amused. Instead of looking forward to *Wonderful World* five albums later, I was dreading it. And it wasn't only Winters. Why, I wondered, in a fifty-seven-album rotation, had I seen fit to include nine Cosby albums? With expansion out of the question—I owned everything by everybody who mattered—I was faced with further paring. What would I be left with? Forty albums, one for each year of my life? A Baskin-Robbins Cycle? I flipped through the albums and set aside each that made me wince.

Only three survived the cut.

Many of Bob Newhart's bits sounded dated, even to my ears. His vocabulary was conventional, and he never spiced things up by working blue. He sounded like what he was: a bookkeeper-turned-comedian, just the sort of corporate amateur I had come to despise. But nobody had better characters or better stories than Newhart.

On the live recordings that would become his second record, *Bob Newhart: The Button-Down Mind Strikes Back*, Newhart was so well known and well loved that even his setups got laughs. But when he recorded his debut album, *The Button-Down Mind of Bob Newhart*, at the Tidelands Club in Houston, none of the setups got a snigger, not even the setup of what would become his signature bit, "Abe Lincoln vs. Madison Avenue." As Newhart laid out the Lincoln premise—that if Lincoln had not existed during the Civil War, an enterprising PR mind would have created him—the only sound was that of a woman coughing.

Newhart played a press agent speaking with Lincoln over the phone right before the Gettysburg Address. The audience heard only the press agent's side of the conversation—Newhart would speak and pause to listen, speak again, then pause again to listen—but the Lincoln created around those pauses, a mosaic of the press agent's repetitions and intimations, was utterly convincing. The bit concluded with the press agent taking his leave and ending the call. The only break with story and character was Newhart's raising his voice over the raucous applause.

Absorbing Newhart's subtle clues, I would play a corresponding Lincoln in my head. Initially, I had imagined his voice as the smooth baritone he might have had on a local Presidents' Day-sale commercial, but eventually I settled on something a little higher. I played him crackling with pre-address nerves or, when I heard a hint of deference that suggested the press agent was the nervous one, as a sitting President impatient with a P.R. flak he's starting to think he doesn't need anymore. Because Newhart's performance always offered something to be discovered, I was never the same Lincoln twice.

Any comedian's albums could have drowned out the New Age music wafting up from the day spa beneath my apartment and lent their structure to my life—Newhart's albums helped me to escape it, somehow. Disability paid my rent, and my father brought groceries on Saturdays. As long as my record player and my Newhart records held out, I had everything I needed.

One afternoon I noticed that the New Age music was gone. Was it a holiday? I took a few steps toward the window and looked down on Fullerton Avenue through a gap in the curtains. A crisp orange and white parking ticket was pinned beneath the windshield wiper of a two-door Honda. Not a holiday. Then I moved one of the curtains back and checked the reflection in the glass façade of the medical building across the street. The storefront windows of the day spa had been covered, top to bottom, with overlapping sheets of newsprint.

At first, the vacancy was a boon. With no one below and only the flat roof above, I listened to Newhart sandwiched by silence. Honking motorists and shouting pedestrians made daily incursions, but they didn't last. I reassessed the ideal volume level on my grandmother's player, turning the cylindrical steel knob two graduations to the left, protecting my aged speakers and my aging ears.

When the day spa was still vacant after six months, I congratulated myself. Somehow, I must have known this apartment was the place for me.

Then the workers arrived.

At first, the sounds were those of demolition, the knocking down and tearing out of plaster walls with sledges and hammer claws. The workers seemed to relish the noise. They certainly made no effort to keep it down.

After a few days, demolition gave way to construction. Nail guns injected their ammunition into studs with a hydraulic snap, and a sickening thud I could feel through the seat of my recliner. When a nail gun wouldn't do, the men used their hammers. Power saws tore through two-by-fours, and trowels clanged against the naked concrete floor. Over it all, the foreman barked curt instructions and construction comedians traded double entendres in muffled but distinguishable tones.

Newhart could not compete. The rhythms of his pauses, stutters and stammers were overwhelmed from below by hammering, gunning and cutting. The laughter was always audible, even when saws reduced Newhart to murmuring. But I could no longer hear what the audiences were laughing at.

I had listened to those three Newhart records in chronological order—six spins each, each and every day—for months. Now that doing so was no longer possible, I retreated to my bedroom. It wasn't any quieter in there—it was louder, in fact—but the sight of my grandmother's record player lying idle, the Newhart records stacked on the cherry top, was too much for me, so I sat on the floor in the corner of my bedroom, jumping or twitching at the sound of each shot from a nail gun. My eyes stayed open unless I consciously closed the lids or fell asleep.

After five days of demolition and construction, the workers knocked off at six p.m. on Friday. Silence re-enveloped me, this time with the promise of a sixty-hour respite. Around seven, I opened my bedroom door and padded over the dusty living room floor. As I dialed the only number I ever dialed, motes tumbled at knee level through narrow shafts of evening summer sunlight and disappeared again.

"Hello," my father said.

"Dad?"

"Jimbo! How are you, buddy?"

"Home—home from work already?" My father, a litigator, had celebrated his sixty-fifth birthday recently by announcing he was cutting back his workweek to fifty hours.

"Just walked in the door. Just a second." The receiver clicked against a hard surface and bags rustled in the background. "I picked up some pasta from Vito's on the way home, and I had them box up some eggplant parmesan for you. I'll bring it over tomorrow."

My mother had passed away ten years before, and my father still had no inclination to cook for one.

"Thanks," I said.

"No sweat. So did you hear the news?"

"What news?"

"Newhart signed a book deal."

"Really?"

"'An autobiography,'" my father read from the newspaper crinkling in his hand, "'told thematically rather than chronologically in humorous anecdotes from the long-running career of this national treasure.' Think they're overstating things a bit?"

"Maybe."

"That ought to provide some good bedtime reading for you. Maybe you should work it into the rotation with the records?"

For my father, the fastidiousness with which I stuck to my routine was more troubling symptom than soothing balm.

"I don't think so," I said.

"OK. No pressure. Just a thought. So what's happening?"

"When you come over tomorrow, I'm going to be taking a nap."

"Oh." My father paused. "You feeling all right?"

"I feel fine. Just a little tired." I had sat in the corner of my bedroom an extra half-hour marshaling the energy to answer that question convincingly. I hoped it had been enough. "So if you don't mind, please put the groceries away for me."

"What if I came by at three instead of noon?"

I squirmed. He was handling me the way he had handled my mother once her condition had worsened, assessing my stability and flexibility with questions, giving me a chance to ask for help. I would be hard pressed to convince him I didn't need any.

"I'm not sure I'll be up by three, Dad."

"That's a hell of a nap, Jim."

Though he encouraged minor variations in my routine, my father was deeply suspicious of sweeping changes to it. He had come to accept my condition and my capabilities—he hadn't always—but I suspected he still harbored fears, despite dozens of doctors having assured him they were unfounded, that I was a few bad days from spiraling into what I'd heard him call "outright madness," as if the term were a medical one and my troubles simply madness of some lesser degree.

"You can look in on me," I said. "Just try not to wake me up, OK? I'll call you when I get up." My father made no reply. "Dad, I'm fine."

"What's fine mean?"

"What it usually means." In the silence that followed, I felt myself flagging.

Having asked his questions, my father stopped playing hotline operator and assumed the decisive, authoritative tone he used on business calls. "Call me when you wake up. I'll bring your groceries over then. I'm not a delivery boy. I want to see my son."

"OK, Dad," I said. "I'll be talking to you."

By Monday, I had adjusted to my new schedule. I slid under the covers at six a.m. and was asleep before the construction noise began. Occasionally, a shout or crash or the grind of a circular saw below would cause me to stir, but no more than the Dopplerized sirens of passing ambulances had disturbed my sleep at night. I set the alarm for six p.m., when the workers were cleaning up and clearing out, to allow for six nightly spins of each Newhart record. In short, I reclaimed my life by making days of my nights.

But while I slept, the men below me kept working.

As I woke one evening, I felt my teeth chattering to the frequency of vibrations coming—from where? I rolled over and reached a hand down to the floor. It was shaking, but the vibrations were not coming from below. Were they working on the roof? Then the quaking stopped. I checked the clock. Five-fifty p.m., nearly wake-up time, anyway. I opened the door to my bedroom and peered around its edge.

I see no point in denying that the man in hard-hat and harness rappelling past my living room window scared the hell out of me. I closed the bedroom door and, when the vibrations began again without warning, slid into the corner near the closet for a brief but energetic cry.

A half-hour later, no men were visible through the windows, but the narrow trapezoid of sunlight that moved daily across my floor had been sawed off by the shadow of something opaque and rectangular. With my nose pressed against the frame of the window, I saw the steel supports that the urban mountaineer had drilled into my wall, and the sign they held in the air.

"Basement Laughs?" I whispered.

I looked at the reflection in the façade across the street. The newsprint covering the windows of the day spa had been replaced by plastic printed with a red brick wall pattern. Greasepaint letters on the glass read, "The Comedy

Starts July 10th!"

That same night, the Basement Laughs staff tested the new sound system. That the bass thumped and rumbled throughout my apartment was unsurprising, as low-end noise from the trunks of passing cars often penetrated my walls. But I hadn't expected the ear-splitting power of the treble. I heard each cymbal crash, synthesizer note and lead-vocal scream with piercing clarity; they might as well have put a speaker in my living room. I stared at my grandmother's record player. Up against the Basement Laughs system, Newhart would sound as if he were performing with a cheerleader's megaphone during a sold-out rock concert.

With the construction job more or less complete, I tried to reverse my sleeping pattern again, but I could neither sleep nor stay awake the twenty or so hours it would have taken to rejoin the night-sleepers. So I slept during the day and awoke to endure more sound checks, wondering what silent waking hours would be left to Newhart and me once the club opened and—the thought made me shudder—they started doing stand-up.

Once the club opened, I discovered that the bass and treble could be ignored. The comedy, however, could not. Basement Laughs hosted open-mike nights on Monday, Tuesday and Wednesday. Amateurs indistinguishable in their lack of talent filled the slots. They were the sort of figures who had nearly ruined stand-up in the late 80s: new moms telling jokes about minivans and dirty diapers, sales reps skewering (in their own minds, anyway) the stuffiness of corporate America.

After a few weeks, the arrhythmia of these open mikers

had clogged me. I no longer remembered what good stand-up felt like, and I reacted viscerally to the bad, running my hands through my hair, pacing a tight oval in the living room, even groaning aloud. One night, a would-be comic kept taking a pause every time he thought he deserved a laugh, but the audience wasn't going for it. Near the end of his set, after an elaborate setup about sexual-harassment training, he said, "I guess I don't understand. I thought we were *supposed* to be 'getting a-head' at work."

As the beat swelled with mirthless silence, I dropped to my knees and pounded my fists into the floor. "Idiot!" I screamed. "People don't laugh when you pause! They laugh when you're funny! You're not funny!"

When cleanup was done, usually around four a.m., the Basement Laughs staff would cut the music, leaving me around two hours of silence before I fell asleep. I would hold the edges of my Newhart records in my palms and watch the yellow overhead light reflect off the grooved, black wax. But I couldn't play them any more than a gourmet, having been force-fed fast food, could sit down to a seven-course French meal. As the sky brightened to gray, I would sit in my recliner hoping silence would clear my head and fix me. It failed on both counts.

Without wanting to, I eventually connected one open-mike voice with a name. Tony Cascarino took the Basement Laughs stage every Monday, Tuesday *and* Wednesday to tell unrelated jokes in a clipped yuppie patter. At first I thought he might have been trying to lampoon the character-less, story-less, soulless comics of stand-up's Dark Age. But after a couple of weeks, it became clear to me that Tony was emulating them in earnest. He was doing what he thought a comedian was supposed to do.

And he was doing it badly.

When Tony got nervous, the yuppie patter fell apart and his Italian city-kid accent took its place. One night he did a bit—it could've been a story, but it wasn't—about working at a dot-com. "The touchy-feeliest place I ever worked," Tony said. "First day on the job, they showed me to my desk, pulled out an ergonomic desk chair and said, 'Make yourself dot-comfortable.'" That line got one chuckle, probably from some guy who couldn't stand the silence after a dud. It was the only laugh Tony got that night. And by the time he delivered a joke about being fired via mix tape, Tony's yuppie sounded like a goombah caricature.

After Tony had been doing open mikes for about a month, some of the Basement Laughs regulars started cheering raucously each time he was introduced. They'd quiet down to let him begin, but then, as Tony tried desperately to set up his first punch line, one of them would shout his name, and the others would join in, whooping and clapping. When they had gotten to him, the cheering section would clam up and let Tony bake under the lights in silence. In the absence of any humor on stage, the Basement Laughs regulars were supplying their own—making Tony the joke.

Yet, in the face of certain harassment, Tony Cascarino still went on every Monday, Tuesday and Wednesday night. He had no local following to build on, no headlining gig or tour or TV deal on the horizon. But he kept coming back.

Any comedian will tell you that you've got to want it bad to get good. Tony wanted it bad.

If I had been able to see his expression and his body language, I would have known for certain. Upstairs in my apartment, all I could do was guess. Maybe he was heading his hecklers off at the pass. Maybe his confidence was shot before he took the stage. Whatever the reason, Tony Cascarino didn't draw from his dot-com and cubicle material that Tuesday night. And from the moment he took the mike, he spoke like the Italian city kid I assumed he really was.

"All right everybody, how we doin'?"

Tony's heckler friends screamed his name, but he spoke right over them.

"That's great. Excellent. So I was driving down the Interstate the other day on the way to my ma's house and I saw this billboard for Tuggzie's. You guys know Tuggzie's? Home of the Tallburger and whatnot?"

Over the murmurs and claps that indicated most of the audience had indeed heard of the hamburger chain, two people shouted Tony's name. He paid them no mind.

"So I see this billboard for Tuggzie's and it says, 'Sooner or later you know you want it.'"

Tony paused. I imagined him shrugging in confusion.

"'Sooner or later you know you want it,'" he repeated. "What the hell is 'it?' There's no photo of the Tallburger or a Tuggzie's shake. It looked to me like the ad guys had cribbed the line from *Date Rape for Dummies*. If that line gets people to buy burgers, maybe GM should use 'But I bought you dinner!' to sell cars!"

For the rest of the set, Tony told broad, bad jokes like that one. But, for the first time, he didn't tell them the way he thought they were supposed to be told. He told them in a voice he was able to pull off—his own. With the city-kid accent and the driving-to-ma's-house setup, Tony had managed to inhabit, well, a stereotype. While I knew that the odds were stacked against Tony ever getting from stereotype to character, he had already come further than I had ever thought possible.

I found myself rooting for Tony, mostly for selfish reasons—I was a captive audience and I wanted a good show. It didn't have to be perfect, and it didn't have to be Tony, but I wanted ten minutes—just *ten minutes*—of character and story from a comic with even a journeyman's sense of timing. The night I got that, I would be able to listen to Newhart when the jam stopped pumping at four a.m. But tonight—this morning—I could only shuffle my slippered feet over the hardwood floor, crawl into bed, and wait for sleep.

The next night, a Wednesday, Tony took two steps back. He performed the same jokes with tweaks ("maybe GM should use 'Look at the way you're dressed!' to sell cars!") that failed to improve them. His only new joke had something having to do with an HIV-positive Muppet and Kermit the Frog giving warts to a character named Elmo. I gave Tony the benefit of the doubt and assumed I hadn't watched enough Sesame Street to get the joke. Judging from the groans, the audience got the joke and hated it.

The following Monday, I waited patiently for the emcee to introduce Tony. By ten-thirty, he had not been announced. I hadn't gotten the ten solid minutes I needed from the prop comic who had headlined the previous weekend, and none of tonight's open mikers had come close. I would have taken the ten minutes from anyone capable of giving them, but as the emcee took the mike at ten to eleven to introduce the final open miker of the night, I realized that I wanted those ten minutes from Tony, as much for him as for myself.

"How about another round of applause for Jeremy Folsom," the emcee said.

The audience obliged the request mechanically.

"All right," he continued. "Thanks from all of us here at Basement Laughs for coming out tonight. In just a few minutes, local sensation Nick Jovanovich will be out here for you."

More polite applause, plus some whooping from those I assumed to be Nick Jovanovich's friends and family.

"So stick around for that. We'll have open mikes tomorrow and Wednesday night, followed by more from Nick Jovanovich. And on Thursday night, we'll welcome Jake Teelander back to the Basement Laughs stage."

One man whooped.

"Then on Friday, Saturday and Sunday, Basement Laughs will have two shows, at eight-thirty and eleven, with Brian Posehn."

The audience seemed to recognize the name and cheered approvingly.

"He'll be fresh off an appearance on the *Late Late Show*, so get your tickets as you leave tonight," he continued. "It's going to be a great show. Doors open at seven-thirty.

"OK! Once again, thank you for coming out to Basement Laughs. We'll hope to see you this weekend. And now, without further ado, our final open-mike performer of the evening. Ladies and gentleman, let's have a big hand for Mr. Tony Cascarino."

As Tony took the stage to the faux excitement of the

heckling regulars, I scooted up to the edge of my recliner. I had no real notion of the club's layout, but I imagined Tony was standing almost directly below me. I stared at the floor and listened.

"All right, everybody, how we doin' tonight?" Tony began. Even as the applause died, one guy was still shouting his name. "That's terrific. All right. So I go over to my ma's house for lunch on Saturday like I usually do, and when I get there, there's this woman at the table. A woman besides my mom, all right, smart ass?"

Tony had put a little menace in his voice for this last line and had gotten a small laugh. I hadn't heard any smart-ass comments from the audience. Had Tony invented a heckler?

"So my ma introduces this woman to me, says her name is Rita and that she'll be joining us for lunch. Now Rita's nice, a few years younger than me, maybe, and attractive. And, given who I am and who my ma is, I'm smelling set-up, right?"

The audience murmured its agreement.

"Right. So we make small talk for a while, and then ma says she has to go upstairs for a minute, which she never does with food on the stove. So she leaves Rita and me alone." Tony paused for a beat. "And Rita goes to guns. I mean, she starts grilling me, asking me about my job, what school I went to, what kind of car I drive. Can you believe that? What kind of car I drive? I'm like, 'What is this, L.A.? I drive a Crown Vic and it gets me to my ma's place and Soldier Field and back. What else do you need in Chicago?'"

I rolled my eyes and sat back in my chair, but the audience cheered. With the dig at L.A. and the reference to the home of the Chicago Bears, Tony had gone for easy affirmation and gotten it. I was disappointed, but, given the kind of sets Tony had been having, I could hardly blame him for pandering.

Then it occurred to me that the rah-rah Chicago stuff might have a more legitimate purpose: what if Tony was trying to put some flesh on the bones of his Italian city-kid stereotype? Though that reasoning had been (quite literally) imposed on his act from above, it seemed possible—for the first time—that Tony might actually know what the hell he was doing.

"Then Rita asks me what my type is," Tony continued. "And I'm like, 'O-positive.'"

A few audience members snorted.

"That's about how funny she thought it was, too."

That got a laugh, but Tony spoke over it, maintaining his rhythm, showing a glimmer of the confidence the good ones had.

"But she keeps after it and says, 'Come on. What's your type?' So I try to be honest with her. I say, 'Well, you know, I have a few things I like—dark brown hair, bright blue eyes, a woman with some heft to her—but I don't really have a type.' I try to leave it at that, but she tells me to go on, and I say, 'I guess it's like those Supreme Court judges said about pornography. I know it when I see it.' And, frankly, she likes the line. And the porno reference doesn't throw her, which is nice."

More laughter.

"So she's sending all the right signals—putting her hair behind her ears, smiling, all that good stuff. But my brain's working overtime on my type, the Supreme Court, all kinds of things I don't usually think about, and I say, out loud, but mostly to myself, 'That's not the only way my type is like pornography."

This busted them up. Legitimately. I felt the laughter rumble through my chair.

"Anyway," Tony said over an exhalation, "she left after that."

And the laughter swelled again.

"So my ma comes down as I'm finishing my sausage and peppers and says, 'Where's Rita?' And I say, 'She left, Ma.' Of course, she immediately assumes I said something to blow it, and she's clickin' her tongue at me and mumbling under her breath, either swearin' at me or prayin' for me, I can never tell."

The laughter for that line was knowing, as if the audience could see Tony's mother behaving in just the way he'd described.

"So I go over to the pot to get another sausage and she says to me, 'How many of those have you had?' And I say, 'Just one, Ma.' Then she looks at my glass and says, 'How many glasses of wine?' And this hurts me deeply."

The audience laughed at the disingenuousness of the remark. I pictured Tony putting his hand over his heart as he said it, and smiled.

"So I say, 'Ma! Come on! Just one! It's like you say, all things in moderation, right?' And she says, 'That doesn't mean you should be drunk half the time!'"

It was a hackneyed line, but because he gave it to the mother—the mother character!—it got a laugh.

Before the laugh had died, Tony said, "You guys have been great. G'night."

And with that, the set was over.

I was too astonished to applaud. The material was C-level at best, but Tony had converted his Italian stereotype into a real character by telling a story. And he hadn't sacrificed timing to anything, not even to the laughs he'd surely been desperate to hear in such quantity and quality.

At three-thirty, when the last one out locked Basement Laughs up for the night, I kept my seat for a moment, relishing a silence I could finally fill. Then I pulled *The Button-Down Mind of Bob Newhart* from its sleeve, laid it gently on the turntable and set it spinning. I counted thirty-three revolutions, then put the needle in the groove at the record's edge. Even before I heard Newhart introduced by the Tidelands emcee, I knew how I would play Lincoln that night. After all this time, Abe must have missed the sound of his press agent's voice almost as badly as I did.

The next night, Tony did the same lunch-at-ma's routine and the hecklers let him have it. I listened with my head in my hands as he rushed the setup and laughed nervously at his own jokes. Before Tony could deliver the pornography punch line, a woman shouted it out. Then I heard the bassy thump of the mike hitting the floor, followed by the voice of the emcee announcing the next open miker. He had bombed before, but Tony had never walked out in the middle of a set.

After Basement Laughs closed for the evening, I played two cuts from *The Button-Down Mind Strikes Back*. But I couldn't listen to Newhart—I couldn't even hear him because I was replaying Tony's miserable set in my head over and over, continually reliving the moment he left the stage. That Tony had reached his breaking point was clear. But had he stalked off defiantly, with his chin set and his head held high, or had he shielded crying eyes from his tormentors?

I knew that the empathy I had developed for Tony was the stuff of the amateur aficionado, not the seasoned connoisseur, but that knowledge didn't help me. I felt what I felt. And Tony's disaster, so close on the heels of his triumphant metamorphosis, destroyed what little of my routine I had managed to salvage.

Dear Tony,

Congratulations on your set this past Monday evening. It was very well done. Your development of story and character has helped your act immensely, and the many laughs you received were well deserved.

I understand that when you performed last night (Tuesday), things did not go as well. Though such an experience is certainly not any fun, I hope you can take some comfort in its universality. All stand-ups—even the great ones—have had a set like that one. They never forget it, but they get past it.

I am not a stand-up comedian. I cannot take the stage, as you do, so I offer the following advice in a spirit of humility. As you continue to develop story and character in your act, you are wise to use open-mike nights as a testing ground. However, when tweaking your material, you might consider working in front of audiences less familiar with it.

If, in making the open-mike circuit, you decide that performing at Basement Laughs still has value for you, I would encourage you, by all means, to return. I would certainly be glad if you did. But I humbly suggest that, at this point in time, your act would be best served by your taking it elsewhere.

Working Chicago clubs on weeknights, you are not likely to encounter many comics worth emulating. Please find the enclosed three albums, each one worthy of emulation from beginning to end. If you listen with an ear for character and story, I'm confident you'll hear something worth applying to your own material.

Congratulations again, and good luck.

Sincerely,

James Ryan

I asked my father to set the package outside the Basement Laughs door at the end of his next Saturday visit. The moment after I handed him the large manila envelope, I grabbed it back and scratched out the return address I had written in the upper left corner. It seemed suddenly important that no one, least of all Tony, know where I lived. My proximity to Basement Laughs invited all sorts of unpleasant questions, none of which I felt much like answering.

As I watched my father walk to his car without the envelope, I realized that I had sent the records around which I had built my life, in care of the club that had nearly ruined it, to a comedian I might never hear again.

I quickly plotted to undo what I had done. No one would arrive to open the club for another half-hour. I could retrieve the records and the letter without seeing anyone, and without anyone seeing me. But at the thought of crossing my threshold and stepping down those stairs, I gagged. I burst through the door—the bathroom door—fell to my knees and clutched the rim of the toilet.

The package might as well have been halfway around the world. It was outside my apartment.

I spent the next several nights anxiously waiting for the performers to be announced—waiting for Tony. I would wonder if he were down there, trying to stay out of sight at the bar or a back table, listening, convincing himself that the material he had been working on was as good as—maybe even better than—anything he heard from the comics performing that night. Then, when the show was over and Tony hadn't performed, I would wait out the music, trying to muster the will to get up from my chair and walk back to bed.

When he delivered the groceries the following Saturday, my father got the sense that something was wrong—something more than the usual. As he left, he announced he would be stopping by each Tuesday and Friday evening, in addition to his regular Saturday visit. Even with nothing to do, I resented the intrusion, but I didn't have the will to stop it.

He would arrive around seven-thirty, dressed in the gray or dark blue suit he had worn to work that day. Once I had let him in, he would not allow me to reclaim my seat until I'd taken a shower. Meanwhile, he would set up a folding chair (the recliner was the only chair in my living room) and open the newspaper, which he would spend most of his visit reading. Though on occasion he would have to raise his voice over the music warming up the Basement Laughs crowd, my father never mentioned the club or the noise.

Damp and exhausted, I would return to the recliner to face an oral account of the previous day's events.

"Alabama was hit by a hurricane," my father said one Tuesday.

"Huh."

"Hurricane Cameron." He paused, reading. "You think that's a good name for a fighter?"

"Sure," I said, rubbing my eyes.

"Heavyweight or lightweight?"

I leaned my head back and let it loll toward the wall.

"Jim?"

"Yeah," I said, turning my head a few degrees in my father's direction.

"Do you think Hurricane Cameron is a better name for a heavyweight or a lightweight?"

"Lightweight, I guess."

"That's what I'd say, too," he said. He turned the page, folding the full-format section in half. Then he chuckled and glanced at me. I recognized my father's pleasure at having come up with a line and his sheepishness at having found it so amusing. He held the newsprint up to give me a clear view of the page's top headline. "'Machine Gun Sales' isn't such a bad name, either."

At eight-thirty, when the emcee introduced the first open-mike performer or opening act, my father would fold up his newspaper, pat me on the shoulder, and leave without a word.

I was still in bed that Friday afternoon when I heard footsteps on the stairs. I checked the clock. My father wasn't due to arrive for another two hours. I crawled on hands and knees into the corner of my bedroom. As the footsteps reached the landing outside my door, I shut my eyes and sank my teeth into my forearm. A moment later, the intruder walked back down the stairs.

I peeked around the bedroom doorframe to find a pale blue, rectangular piece of paper lying on the floor by the front door. Sunlight revealed the swath it had cut through the dust as it slid across the hardwood. As I reached down to pick up the paper, blood trickled out of a tooth mark on my arm.

It was a flyer from Basement Laughs, good for one drink and free admission to a show. Walking toward the trashcan, I skimmed the lineup of comedians for the coming weekend— Tony's name was in tiny print at the bottom of Friday's bill, just above the flyer's heavy black border.

I could only assume that he had been asked to fill in for a local opener who'd had to cancel. But how, and why? Had the Basement Laughs booking manager seen Tony at another club's open mike? Had Tony dropped off video of a good set? The whole scenario was incredible: Tony was returning to Basement Laughs that very night—with a paying gig!

I called my father and asked him not to come over. I told him the truth: a favorite comedian of mine was going on early that night and I would be too nervous to be good company. Perhaps, in the short pause he took, my father wondered if nerves accounted for my having rarely been good company of late. If he wondered, he didn't do it aloud.

"Enjoy the show, Jim," he said. "I'll see you tomorrow."

For the first time in weeks, I showered without coercion. I hadn't had many big nights of late, and I wanted at least to be clean for this one. After toweling off, I stood in front of my closet and stared at my lone pair of dress slacks. In that moment, I considered going downstairs. Twenty-five steps. Twenty-five steps and I would be watching Tony's triumphant return to the Basement Laughs stage. And my presence might actually do some good. Most of the people seated in time to see Tony would likely have no interest in him—he was the low man on the bill, after all. They would have arrived early simply to secure a good seat for the headliner. They would order drinks and whisper as Tony performed, enduring his set instead of enjoying it. Tony needed someone in the audience who was actually there to see him.

What he didn't need, however, was someone running for the door in the middle of his set and throwing up in front of the bouncer. And that, despite my best intentions, would be all I had to offer.

So I put on a button-down shirt and my dress slacks—it was still a special evening—poured myself a glass of water and settled into my recliner. Waiting for Tony to be announced, I leaned forward and fidgeted with my cuffs, buttoning and unbuttoning them.

At eight-thirty on the dot, the music faded and the emcee took the mike. "Good evening, folks, and welcome to Basement Laughs."

The audience applauded dutifully.

"We've got a great show for you tonight, so we're going to get right to it. Our first comic is new to the professional ranks, though if you've been to open mikes around town, you might have caught his act *in media res*, which is Latin for 'when it sucked.'"

The line was good-natured and it got a laugh. I imagined Tony just offstage, probably nervous as hell, managing to crack a smile.

"How about a big hand for Tony Cascarino."

Tony took the stage to polite applause. I heard an amplified thud—he was pulling the mike out of its stand. Good, I thought. He isn't trying to hide behind the mike stand.

"All right, everybody how we doin' tonight?" he said. "That's great. Glad to hear it. So my brother calls me a month or two ago and tells me his eleven year-old kid wants to play football."

Tony had barely taken a breath between the salutation and the setup. He was rushing. I leaned further forward. Anxiety tightened my stomach like a drumhead.

"Not flag football." Tony said. "Full-pad, full-contact football for kids. Like the NFL, but more intense."

The juxtaposition earned Tony a light chuckle he pretended he didn't want.

"No! This Pop Warner shit is serious. It's supposed to be a recreational activity for kids. But these coaches are crazy. Parents, you put complete control of the minds and bodies of your children into the hands of these men, and they bring the shit from their jobs, from their dads, from their own playing days, and lay it on the size-small shoulder pads of your little Mikey, a hundred-pound running back who runs a seven-four forty."

That laugh sounded different than the previous one—not louder, but somehow deeper. Then it hit me. Only the men had laughed.

"What the hell were our parents thinking dropping us off at the park with these guys and just taking off? I mean, when I played Pop Warner—any of you guys play football when you were kids? Before high school?"

A smattering of applause. I started to worry. If Tony thought he could have a good set speaking only to the men in the audience, he was wrong.

"OK, some of you did, too. Did any of you guys have to do what they call an 'Indian Run?'"

Tony inhaled sharply through clenched teeth, seemingly aping the reaction of those audience members who had done an Indian Run.

"Yeah. Brings back memories, doesn't it? For those of you whose parents weren't idiots, an Indian Run"—he spoke right over the chuckles—"involves lining up a whole team of players—thirty, forty kids—single file and starting them on a slow jog around the perimeter of a football field. The maniac coach stands at the fifty-yard line and blows his whistle every thirty seconds or so. When he does, the guy at the back of the line has to sprint from the back of the line to the front. And what's he got to do as he runs up there, fellas?"

A man shouted Hollywood Indian war whoops. The audience laughed.

"That's right," Tony said. "Relax, everybody. The wagon train's safe. You can go back to sleep, all right?"

The audience laughed again. I realized then that Tony's Italian city kid was different. He was smarter now.

Though the laughs were coming from men and women now, I was still worried. Tony was mired in the setup. He clearly had a story to tell, but he hadn't started telling it yet and he was five minutes into a fifteen-minute set. No wonder he had rushed at the top.

"So you got a bunch of kids running around whooping like Oglala Sioux warriors. Now, those of you who haven't heard of the Indian Run before, I know what you're thinking: dwarf tossing would be a less offensive way to get in shape. Maybe some of the entrepreneurs in the audience are thinking of sponsoring a politically incorrect pentathlon: Indian run, dwarf toss, anorexic javelin . . ."

I smiled and rearranged my haunches on the seat cushion as the audience laughed. Tony was employing a technique of the masters. He had invented audience members—the entrepreneurs—and pinned the politically incorrect material on them. With the straw men to bear the stigma, Tony could tell whatever joke he wanted and the audience would be free to laugh. But the jokes still had to be funny.

"Pole vault and broad jump wouldn't even need new names."

The laughter gave me a jolt, as it must have Tony. The audience was laughing despite itself. Most of them had paid the cover to enjoy that loss of control, but they probably hadn't expected to enjoy it before they had finished their second drink.

Though the pentathlon tangent had worked, the pressure to pay off the football setup was building.

"My Pop Warner coach had a name, but none of us knew it," Tony said. "To his face, we called him 'Sir.' Outside of earshot, we used the nickname his assistants had given him: 'The Colonel.' The Colonel wore jeans, a white t-shirt, and an army jacket. Every night. When the Colonel raised his arm to point out a defensive formation, you cursed yourself for being five feet tall. Taller would've been great, but shorter would've been fine, too. Anything to get your head out of the pits of that jacket."

Tony had found a rhythm. The audience was laughing—quietly, but in all the right places. More importantly, they were listening to the story. Tony had them. I hoped he knew what to do with them.

"The Colonel's service in Vietnam—where, by the way, there's no way he was a colonel—played out across every part of our football team. He called the starting offensive and defensive units 'platoons,' and special teams were 'special ops.' The Colonel called a long forward pass an 'air strike.' Everybody already called a long forward pass a 'bomb,' but apparently that wasn't good enough for the Colonel.

"And what did he call the drill that every other football coach in the Midwest called the Indian Run?" Tony paused for effect. "'The Ho Chi Minh Trail.'" Tony plowed right through the laughter. "We'd line up single file and start jogging. The Colonel, standing at the fifty-yard line, would yell 'Ambush!' and the eleven year-old in the back would sprint to the front screaming Asian gibberish."

Tony was playing it straight, almost deadpanning it, but the audience was laughing hysterically.

"The kid who played left cornerback for us was named Panh Nguyen. He didn't seem to mind much, but I bet his parents would've preferred we call it the Indian Run. But it makes sense, if you think about it. The Colonel fought in Vietnam, we ran the Ho Chi Minh Trail. Who coached you Indian Run guys, General Custer?"

Tony allowed himself a brief laugh along with the audience. I checked my watch. About seven minutes left.

"It was the Colonel who told me I'd been wiping my ass all wrong."

Though only a setup, the line got a laugh.

"Seriously. I was a wide receiver, and on the Colonel's team, everybody except the quarterback got into a three-point stance. One day in practice, I ran out to my spot and stood up during the snap count, like the receivers do in the pros. The Colonel blows his whistle, I look over, and he's staring right at me. 'Cascarino!'" Tony growled into the mike. "'Get down in your stance! Son of a—do you wipe your ass standing up?'"

Tony milked the nervous silence. When he spoke again, he sounded like an addict finally able to admit he has a problem.

"I don't know why I wiped my ass standing up."

Understanding—indicated with laughter and applause—seemed to move over the audience like a wave.

"Until the Colonel asked me that, I thought everybody did it standing up. I must have learned to do it that way when I was so small I would've fallen into the bowl if I'd tried it sitting down and then, you know, old habits . . ."

He trailed off beneath the laughter. Despite the results, I was a little disappointed that Tony had gone scatological. I had been around long enough to know that stand-up was a gritty art form, and that bodily functions were fair game. But for me, aesthetically speaking, scatological humor didn't work unless it was an integral part of a larger story's arc. To me the ass-wiping material felt more like a detour for an easy laugh. It felt cheap.

Tony had five minutes left. It was enough time to tie the

scattered set together, but I reminded myself that, at this stage in his development, Tony probably couldn't close. I marveled at how quickly I had raised my expectations and ratcheted them back down.

"So anyway, my brother decides to let his kid—my nephew, Jerry—play football. I say, 'Tommy, you didn't play Pop Warner. These coaches are crazy.' And my brother starts telling me that Jerry really loves football, all his friends are doing it, it'll keep him out of trouble—he gives me every justification in the book, and I'm like, 'Tom, if you want out of your Saturday morning chores, take up golf.' But he doesn't listen, and he drops Jerry off at the first practice.

"That same night, my brother calls me up and tells me Jerry's psyched because the coach told him he'll be playing quarterback, and that the kid went to bed cuddling a football because the coach said that'll improve his hands. And I say, 'That's great, Tom,' you know, 'Great news.' Then Tommy says, 'Whaddya call that drill they do at the end of practice?' 'What drill?' I said."

It was a phone bit. He'd listened to the Newhart albums! But Tony was giving the audience both sides of the conversation, probably because the brother was more convenience than character.

"'The one where they jog single file and the kid in the back runs to the front.' 'Oh,' I say, 'and they make Indian noises?' And Tom says, 'They don't sound like Indian noises.'"

Tony took a pause here, and someone—it sounded like a woman—giggled and clapped. At least one person had guessed where the bit was going.

"'Well, what do they sound like, Tom?' And Tom says,

'Like Ewoks.' 'Like *Ewoks*, Tom?' 'I don't know, they look like Ewoks who joined the Marines.' 'But what do they sound like, Tom? What kind of noises are they making?' Tom, to his credit, took a second to think about it. 'They sounded . . . Asian.'"

With everyone in on the bit, Tony went nuts.

"He was still coaching! I mean, can you believe it? I returned my pads to the park district almost twenty years ago! And now he's coaching my nephew? I mean, how old is this guy? Hadn't anybody complained? Why hadn't my parents said anything? Why hadn't Panh Nguyen's parents said anything? Hadn't anybody put it together that only kids who'd played for the Colonel showed up at high school calling opposing players Gooks?"

Tony had energized the room. I could feel it through the floor.

"So I tell my brother it's the Colonel, that he should do whatever he's got to do to get Jerry on another team, and that if he can't switch teams, he's got to quit. My brother calls the league commissioner, asks if his son can switch teams, the guy says no, league policy, blah-blah, so my brother does the tough thing—the right thing—and tells the kid he's gotta wait until next year."

The audience expressed its sympathy.

"I know," Tony said. "How do you think I felt? It was partly my fault. If it weren't for me, the kid would be out there playing quarterback, barking signals at the line like a second lieutenant calling in strike coordinates."

The Vietnam stuff was still playing, but it wouldn't play forever. I hoped Tony wouldn't overdo it.

"The kid was upset, and knowing the Colonel as I did,

I knew my nephew wasn't the only one. He's quick, big for his age, and he can throw pretty well. The Colonel had told the kid he was going to play quarterback after one practice, so I knew he'd noticed. But what did I care?" Tony was defiant. "I'm 31 years old. I've got a life of my own, and my nephew's welfare to think about. I can't be worrying about some lunatic coach's hard feelings over an eleven year-old quitting his team.

"Then the phone rings."

The audience laughed and clapped in anticipation.

"Hello?"

Pause.

"Speaking."

Pause.

"Who?"

Pause.

"Yeah?"

Pause.

"Do I know you?"

Then Tony snapped to attention.

"Yes, sir, I remember you now."

Pause.

"Did they call you that, sir? I'm not sure I ever heard that."

The audience laughed approvingly.

"No, sir, I never called you that."

Pause.

"Not once. Not ever."

I knew then that Tony had gotten the albums, and that he had studied them. Just for a moment, I tore myself from the world of Tony's act, looked up at the walls of my apartment, and enjoyed an awareness of my present: I was listening to Tony Cascarino do a one-sided phone call, a conversation between two full-blooded characters who were part of a compelling story. And it was killing.

"What can I do for you, sir?"

Pause.

"Yes, sir, I know him. He—he's my nephew."

I heard more than the character's nervousness in Tony's stammer. I heard a conscious homage to Newhart.

"Yes, sir, I heard he left the team."

Pause.

"No, what reason did he give?" Tony managed a nervous laugh. "That was the reason my nephew gave?"

Pause.

"No, no."

Pause.

"No, of course, sir, I believe you. I just can't picture my nephew saying he had to quit because his Dad's a pussy."

Pause.

"Something to that effect. OK. I see what you mean."

I didn't know the Colonel well enough to play him as I would have played Lincoln, but I could get in a room with him. I watched undetected as the Colonel sat in an old recliner not unlike my own, his right wrist perched on an old wooden end table, the smoke from his cigarette carrying up through yellow lamplight.

"Excuse me, sir," Tony said, "but I—I'm wondering why you called to tell me this."

Pause.

"You want me to convince him to rejoin the team."

Pause.

"I don't think I can do that, sir. I'm not his father."

Pause.

"Well, that means I can't tell him what to do."

Pause.

"I realize that, sir, but you were in the army, and he outranked you, sir."

The biggest laugh yet! But then Tony took a pause so long that the laughter died out completely. A chair scraped across the floor. A woman coughed. I felt my toes curling under themselves. Had Tony forgotten his place? Was he searching for the next line?

"Say something!" I yelled.

"I don't think that's going to work, sir," Tony said, at last.

Pause.

"Well, for one thing, I don't have a sniper rifle."

Pause.

"Even if I borrowed yours, sir, I wouldn't know how to shoot it."

Pause.

"Really, I—I couldn't ask you to do that, sir. You've taught me so much already."

I shook my head slowly and felt myself smile as the audience laughed. Tony had gotten into a good story. I hoped he could get out of it.

"I hate to say it, sir, but I don't think there's anything I can do except convince my brother to let my nephew play next year."

Pause.

"I know he'll go back in the draft, sir, but you'll have a good shot of getting him again."

Pause.

"Exactly, sir," Tony said, brightening. "So how's the rest of the team look?"

Pause.

"Is that bad?"

Pause.

"I'm sorry, sir, I didn't get the reference. Everything I know about Vietnam I learned from *Platoon* and *Apocalypse Now* and—and I haven't seen them in a while, sir."

The balance of power had shifted. The Tony character was controlling the conversation now. It was his to end and time to end it.

"It was nice to hear from you, sir. Oh, and sir? I meant what I said before—that you'd taught me a lot."

The tone of the entire conversation had been ironic, but, somehow, Tony had managed to strike a sincere note.

"No, sir," Tony said. "Sitting down. Ever since you asked me the first time."

And with that line, Tony transformed his rocky scatological detour into a paved Victory Lane. The ass wiping had been integrated into the arc of a story that spanned decades, and that, to my mind, was all it took to redeem both the material and the man who delivered it.

Having sewn up the plot points, Tony hung up with the Colonel and said goodnight over the audience's cheers. People were still applauding and whooping—not like Indians or Asians, but like themselves—when the emcee took the microphone.

"Tony Cascarino, ladies and gentlemen!"

The applause swelled again. I dropped to my knees, pounded my appreciation into the hardwood with my fists, and let out a long, single-note whoop. When I'd run out of breath, I rolled over and sat on the floor.

I looked at my hands. The outsides were deep red and the palms were marked where I had dug in my fingernails. While the emcee introduced the next comedian, I ran cold water over my hands. Then I shut the water off, rested my forearms on the edge of the kitchen counter and leaned against it with one foot stacked on the other and my head bowed. Expressing my appreciation—with more violence, this time, than virtuosity—had exhausted me.

I went to bed while the headliner was still on, but I didn't sleep. I replayed Tony's act in my head, deciphering why it had worked and why, in parts, it hadn't. And as I lay there, I realized for the first time that I had nothing against jokes. Really, who could hate a good joke? But even the best joke couldn't do what Newhart—and now Tony—could do with character and story. Playing one of Newhart's characters, or standing alongside one of Tony's, gave me what I wanted most in the world: a way out of my apartment.

IN MEMORIAM

Abe walked to Agata & Valentina to get his coffee. The six blocks down First Avenue between his apartment and the café felt more like four—on the way there, anyway. On the way back, he stopped at a newsstand to catch his breath and pick up a *Times*. The autumn air was crisp and burned his lungs, but as he greeted his building's doorman, Abe felt very much like himself.

Riding up in the elevator, Abe regretted having scheduled a doctor's appointment for this afternoon. He'd had a dizzy spell yesterday morning, but he had done his five minutes at the Friars' roast of Trump in the evening and felt fine. If I still feel fine in an hour, Abe thought, I'll call and cancel the appointment. No point in wasting the doctor's time on a case of the jitters.

Abe had been nervous with good reason. He was 83 years old and hadn't performed in nine months. Would he stumble over Trump's chair on the way to the microphone? Would his timing get to the Hilton on time? But Abe needn't have worried. He got the one big laugh he had counted on, right at the top, and a few smaller laughs, as well. During the big one, Abe looked out at the laughing faces, absorbed the trebly din through his hearing aids, and felt distinctly alive.

Abe had been planning today's activity for weeks, well before he had made the doctor's appointment in a panic. The strongest memory he had of his wife's death, apart from the gut-wrenching palpability of her absence, was the amount of clerical work that had been left behind for her survivors. Abe was determined to do as much as he could in advance, so *his* survivors could take care of themselves. He did not have to finish the preparations today, but he would force himself to start them.

But first, Abe sat at his dining room table, drank his coffee, and read the *Times* to see what they had to say about the roast. He read the lede, mainly niceties for Trump and the Friars Club, then scanned the article for his name. There it was, bringing up the rear in a paragraph listing dais "oddities," including *Survivor* winners and a former light-heavyweight fighter. None of Abe's jokes made the article, but the first line of his introduction did: "If Abe Vigoda were alive today . . . ." It was a good line, and Abe had laughed when he heard it. Even now, he managed a wry smile.

Abe put down the paper and picked up a manila folder from the table. The word DEATH was written in black, permanent marker on the filing tab. As he fingered the die-cut nubs on the rounded, bottom corner of the cover, Abe realized he had to urinate. He pushed back from the table, took seven careful steps to the bathroom off the kitchen, and sputtered the contents of his bladder into the toilet, shaking out the last drops before tucking in and zipping up.

It was the third time he had urinated that day. Abe felt no shame about his frequent trips to the bathroom—they were part of getting older—but he was careful not to dribble any urine down his slacks. Outside their proper receptacle, the little yellow drops could erode a man's dignity.

Back at the table, Abe opened the folder and realized that he hadn't separated documents relevant to his actual death from those pertaining to his supposed death. He would have to sort them before doing anything else.

On top was the deed to his burial plot. Maude had wanted to pick the spot while they were still spry enough to walk around the cemetery and find a good one, so they had driven out to Flushing on a Sunday morning in the fall of 1988. They agreed on a tandem plot beneath an old elm tree, so that Donna and the grandkids would always have a landmark amidst the thousands of headstones. Abe remembered Maude insisting that their burial reflect their usual sleeping arrangement: she on the right as they looked from the head of the bed to the foot, he on the left. The notion had given Abe the creeps, but he had acquiesced, figuring he'd be too dead to care when the time came.

By the time Maude died, the elm had died, too. Unable to live with a rotting stump as a landmark, Abe paid for the transplanting of a young sugar maple. As of his last visit to the gravesite, two years ago this February, the maple had grown tall and thick in the trunk. Sap, viscous in the cold air, slid slowly down cracks in the rough bark. Abe dabbed the sticky liquid with his forefinger and tasted it. He hoped the maple would still be spilling sap long after his own funeral, but if beetles could kill that statuesque elm, Abe figured they could kill anything.

Underneath the burial plot deed was an article *People* magazine had published in 1982, five years after Abe's run as Inspector Phil Fish on *Barney Miller* had come to an end. The article referred to Abe as "the late Abe Vigoda." Dozens of people—some frantic, some kidding—had called the day the issue hit newsstands. Whether the callers intended to assuage their fears or bust Abe's chops, the conversations went pretty much the same way.

"Abe?"

"Speaking."

"You're not dead?"

"Not yet."

"Oh thank God. *People* said you're dead."

"I heard."

"But you're not."

"Nope."

"Great!" they'd say. "That's great. So how's life?"

Abe piled clippings from the *Florida Times-Union*, the *Las Vegas Sun* and *Entertainment Weekly* on top of the *People* article. Sent to him by friends and fans over the past twenty years, the articles stated for the record that Abe Vigoda was still alive. He was more famous for not having died than for having lived.

Every six months or so, someone would approach him at the post office or the grocery store and say, "Excuse me. You look just like Abe Vigoda."

"I am Abe Vigoda," Abe would reply.

The person would smile and nod slowly, as if the two of them were in on a joke, then walk away.

Next, Abe pulled an eight-by-ten headshot from the folder. Pictured in front of a pale-green background, Abe wore a rumpled, gray suit with a brown and tan tie cinched around his unbuttoned collar. His hair was thin and gray on top, thick and bristly around the ears. His arms were folded beneath his chest, and he was smiling. Abe had signed thousands of copies of this photo over the years. Given his role in the *Godfather* films, he imagined that most of them had been hung near the entrances of restaurants he'd never been to with "Loved the saltimbocca!" or "Thanks for a great meal, Jimmy!" forged in black ink above his signature. Flipping the photo over, Abe found he had written "For 'In Memoriam' Tribute" on the back.

Abe had studied the "In Memoriam" segment of the Academy Awards ceremony for years. Character actors traditionally scored well on the applause-o-meter, as the audience grasped at its final chance to give an admired craftsman his due. The key factor, Abe had discovered, was the photos' order. During the 2003 tribute, a still of the dearly departed Rosemary Clooney had been applauded appreciatively, but the appreciation had seemed minimal alongside that given the next slide, a headshot of Dudley Moore. The only position Abe considered a sure-winner was last. The producers left up the final stiff's photo a few seconds longer than the rest, and the audience unleashed the torrent of admiration it had been holding in reserve. Abe knew he was a long shot to close the segment. If Mickey Rooney, for example, were to kick it the same year he did, Abe's photo would have to battle it out with the others in the middle of the pack. He looked at the smiling visage of his younger self. I'll go to war with this one, he thought.

Abe put the photo on top of the burial plot deed and picked up a glossy, tri-fold brochure. The cover read, "Riverside Memorial Chapel—Leaders in Funeral Pre-Planning, and a Source of Support to the Jewish People since 1897." Abe had been handed the brochure five months earlier at the funeral of his friend and fellow Friar Alan King, who had died of lung cancer. With the family's blessing, Alan's old pals, both Borscht Belt pioneers and younger comics he had mentored, eulogized the fallen Friar Abbot by remembering his life and times in setups and punch lines.

Jerry Stiller was the first to address the assembled mourners. "Alan wrote some of his best material about his mother," he said. "That makes two of us."

Abe laughed freely with the crowd, stealing glances at King's wife and kids to make sure that they, too, were laughing.

"I first saw Alan perform in a small club downtown," Stiller continued. "He recounted his mother's exasperation at his refusal to go to school, and said, in a faithful rendition of her accent, 'Why don't you go out and learn a trade? Then at least I'll know what kind of work you're out of.'"

Stiller gave King's joke plenty of room, waiting for the laughter to die out before continuing. To some, it might have seemed a sign of respect, and it was. But Abe smelled a setup.

"Anyone who heard Alan tell a joke like that one," Stiller said, "knew exactly what kind of work he was out of."

After each eulogist had done his five minutes, he would conclude with a handful of eloquent words, expressing "in all seriousness" his sadness and his love for Alan and his family. With short sets of comedy followed by bursts of sincere appreciation for the silent guest of honor, the service was more roast than funeral.

Before the burial, Abe ducked into the directors' office to say hello to Lewie Kirschbaum. Lewie had directed Maude's funeral, and Abe made a point to find Lewie and inquire after his family whenever he came to Riverside.

"Shame about Alan," Lewie said.

"It is," Abe said. "Those damn signature cigars."

"He would have been just as funny with a celery stick."

"Funnier."

"Maybe. How've you been, Abe?"

"I've been good. How's Ada?"

"She's great. Kids are great, too," Lewie said, anticipating Abe's next question. He picked up a Riverside brochure and held it out to Abe. "When your time comes, Abe—you know, a second time—I'd be honored to direct your funeral. I'll have the rabbi read the Abraham story from the Torah, draw comparisons between his life and yours, comic descendants as numerous as the stars, the whole thing. What do you say?"

"Are you selling me, Lewie?"

"If not now, Abe, when? No good when you're dead. Besides, you'll need a hell of a real death to measure up to your false one."

The two men laughed. Abe took the brochure, left the chapel, and drove out to Flushing to bury his friend.

Skimming the sales piece now, Abe thought about King's funeral, about Maude's, and about his own. He pulled a yellow Post-it from a pad on the table and stuck it on the brochure's front cover. On the Post-it, he printed in black ink, "Donna, this is the place. Ask Jerry Stiller, Freddie Roman and Jeffrey Ross to speak." Abe wondered if he should add a name to the list. Roman and Stiller were nearly as old as he was. Maybe Caan would do it, he thought.

In late 1970, Abe had flown to L.A. to meet with Francis Ford Coppola, who was considering Abe for the role of Tessio in *The Godfather*. James Caan, who had already been cast as Santino, sat in at Coppola's invitation. The meeting was not an audition, but Abe thought his only shot at getting the part was to make it one. He had never done film work, and he was up against some experienced film actors for the part. Abe knew that if he performed at the meeting and it went bad, it would look like the stunt of a stage actor in over his head, or worse, like grandstanding. But what the hell, he thought. Maybe they like grandstanding out here.

Abe's longtime agent, Ira, had worked back channels for a copy of the script and had come up empty. So he and Abe looked at a few monologues, stuff that would show that Abe could play the taciturn, murderous caporegime from Puzo's novel. In the end, Abe decided, if given the chance, to sink or swim with the Carnival Barker, an audition piece he had written himself. It was an odd choice for a gangster part, but the Barker had gotten Abe the role of John of Gaunt in *Richard II*, so he figured it could work for anything.

Abe entered a stuffy, wood-paneled room on the Paramount lot, shook hands with Coppola and Caan, and sat down across from them. Caan was drinking, paying half-attention. I must be the fifth Tessio he's met today, Abe thought.

"One of my casting directors saw your performance in *The Man in the Glass Booth* at the Royale," Coppola said.

"All six lines?"

"Apparently you did a lot with a little. Enough to catch

her eye, anyway. How did you like working with Harold Pinter?"

"He's a good director," Abe said. "Allows his actors to make choices, but keeps them faithful to the script."

"I would imagine he does," Coppola said, nodding slowly. "Did you audition for him?"

"Yes."

"What did you do?"

With Coppola's permission, Abe moved his chair and made the thirty-six square feet of linoleum his performance space. Caan took a gulp from his drink and sat back, supporting his neck with his right hand. He looked vaguely amused. Abe closed his eyes, took a deep breath, and centered himself. When he opened his eyes, Abe was more than the Carnival Barker. He was the carnival.

"Step right up! See the bearded lady, the monkey child, the mythical unicorn in the flesh! Or, for something more pleasing to the eye, visit the Can-Can Tent for the Parade of Luscious Legs! You sir!" Abe pointed to Caan, who was watching his every move. "Got a lady?"

"Got a few."

"Impress any one of them with tests of strength and skill! Bang the mallet on the target and ring the Strongman's Bell! Topple the bottles with your fastball! Toss a ring around a Floating Frog, and enjoy, as your lady turns you into a prince with a kiss!"

Caan laughed and watched Abe's performance with intense, glassy eyes.

"Wildest wonders of the Western world, and the Orient, too! Visit the Geisha Exhibition just inside these gates, and edify yourself with photographs of the finest women in the

Far East! You sir!" Abe pointed to Coppola. "Got kids?"

"I do," Coppola said.

"Got 'em with you?"

"I do not."

"Then head back home to get 'em, because we won't be here long! This is the final opportunity to give your kids a day they'll always remember, riding the ponies 'round the Rodeo, feeding the goats and chickens in the Petting Zoo, and clowning with the clowns in the Three-Ring Circus! That's right, sir, here today, gone tomorrow, so step right up, step right up!"

Though Abe wasn't finished, he was stopped cold by Caan, who stood up and applauded, saying, "That's great! That is just great." Coppola applauded, too, and Abe took a shallow bow. Caan turned to Coppola and said, "He's got it, right?"

"That was good work," Coppola said.

"He's got the part, right?" Caan said.

"I'll want to see him do something from the script."

"Do Tessio and Santino have any scenes together?"

Coppola scratched his black, bushy beard. "They've got a lot of scenes together, but not much dialogue."

"Do they have any?"

"A little."

"Give it to me," Caan said, opening and closing his hand.

Coppola found an exchange and handed the script to Caan, who ripped out the page, flipped it sideways, and tore it in two with tiny, twisting movements of his thumbs and forefingers. He walked into the linoleum performance space, smiled, and handed Abe the lower half of the page.

"Do you mind?"

"No," Abe said.

"You read the book?"

"Yes."

"Perfect. Sonny just got the location of the meeting between Michael, Solozzo and McCluskey. Tessio knows the place. Ready?"

Caan bowed his head, inhabited Sonny, and went to work. "That's my man in McCluskey's precinct. A police captain's gotta be on call twenty-four hours a day. He signed out at that number between eight and ten. Anybody know this joint?"

"Yeah, sure, I do," Abe said. "It's perfect for us." Abe built his Tessio from the ground up, using the words on the page. He spoke the unsophisticated phrases at a measured clip, with undertones of fury corralled but not controlled. He didn't use an Italian accent. He spoke like the neighborhood New Yorker he was and hoped that would be enough. "A small family place, good food. Everyone minds his business. Pete,"—in lieu of a Clemenza, Abe addressed Coppola— "they got an old-fashioned toilet. You know, the box, and,"—Abe played Tessio searching for the word—"and, ah, the chain-thing." Then the finish, with excitement rippling just below Tessio's cold calculation: "We might be able to tape the gun behind it."

Caan turned to Coppola. "You see?"

"I see," Coppola said.

On the set of the movie, Caan joked with Abe between scenes, putting his arm around him, referring to the two of them as, "The Jews who would be Italian." After *Godfather: Part II*, Abe would call Caan to ask after him, but

Caan always turned the conversation away from himself and back to Abe. "I'm fine, I'm fine. Working. That's it. So what about you, Fish? How's tricks? How's things at the precinct?"

After Caan got divorced, Abe lost track of him. He sent a letter in care of Caan's agent, even called him once at the Playboy mansion, but couldn't reach him. The only time Abe felt he had an idea of what Caan might have been enduring after the divorce, the only time he understood what it was like to have a hole in you that nothing could fill, was the day Maude died.

Caan called Abe the next night.

"Hello."

"Abe?"

"Yeah."

"It's Caan."

Abe's voice broke. He had taken so many of these calls the past two days. "Yeah."

"Abe, I just heard. I'm so sorry."

"Yeah." Abe covered his eyes with his hand, somehow ashamed to cry in front of a man 3,000 miles away.

"I'm so, so sorry."

Then Abe heard Caan let out a sob. The conversation was reduced to an exchange of sniffs and exhalations, until Abe spoke up.

"You method actors and your goddamned empathy."

Caan laughed with two punctuated breaths. Abe laughed through his nose. They sniffed a few more times, thanked one another, and said goodnight.

Caan would do it, Abe decided, holding the funeral brochure in his hand. He would come, and he would speak.

Abe added Caan's name to the Post-it list of eulogists.

Abe looked at the clock. He was scheduled to visit his doctor in an hour and a half. He took stock of himself and decided he felt fine—better, in fact, than he had when he'd first sat down. Recalling his rendition of the Carnival Barker had energized him. He hadn't done the piece in years, but who knew when he might need it again? He wasn't too proud to audition.

But Abe wondered if an 83-year-old could convince in the role. He stood up, stepped around the dining room table, and began to perform for the chairs. He pantomimed a cane and a straw hat. He belted out an organ grinder's song. He roll-called the freaks and trumpeted the wonders. He pulled on men's heartstrings and played on their desires. He kept going, past where Caan had stopped him, to a place he'd never taken the character before, gesticulating to the limits of his range of motion. He improvised, lifting a lady's skirt with his cane and meeting her imagined outrage with a "who me?" countenance. He bargained with newsboys, offering them a penny—all right, all right, two pennies—for every paying customer they delivered. He invented corners of the carnival that had never existed before: the Sky Rider Chair Swing, sure to shake your stomach like a snow globe, and the Box 'n' Match, where men of mettle meet mano a mano with Tommy "Gun" Adams, Jack Dempsey's favorite sparring partner.

When he finished, the armpits of Abe's starched blue oxford shirt were soaked, and he was breathing heavily, like a Broadway dancer at the end of a number. As excitement rippled through his stomach, Abe considered turning the Carnival Barker into a one-man show: toning it down, beefing it up, giving it dynamics. He had never pondered what became of the Barker when the carnival shut down for the night. Did he drag himself back to a trailer? Was the woman awaiting him there his wife? How did he start his day? By taking a shot of whiskey and gargling soda water? Did he ever feel he was getting too old for it all? Did he ever dribble urine down his pants?

I could answer these questions, Abe thought. I know this guy.

He would call Ira and tell him his plan. He'd write the Carnival Barker show and get a small room off Broadway, maybe fifty seats. It would sell out for a few weeks as an oddity, but if it were good, if he wrote it well and gave them hell on stage, the show would outlast the novelty of Abe Vigoda, alive and in person. There would be reviews that would describe him as "ageless" and call the show "uproariously funny." There would be a renewed run. He would move to a bigger theatre or sign a lifetime contract with the small one. The Carnival Barker would be huge!

He would call Ira, but first he would call the doctor's office. Abe wasn't going anywhere this afternoon, except to the closet to get the typewriter.

He picked up the phone and the receiver felt like it weighed fifty pounds. A tingling—no, a burning—radiated down his arm to his fingers and back up, diffusing into his shoulder and down his left side. Abe stared at the phone, held by an arm he no longer seemed to own, except for the burning sensation. He knew the receiver was yellow, but he saw it in a dulled gray, as if he were looking at it through smoked glass.

He dropped the phone and backed into a chair, nearly

tipping it over backwards. Abe sat for ten minutes, laboring to breathe, ignoring the death documents piled on the table.

Even before it ended, Abe knew the attack would pass. And it did, slowly. The burning in his arm dissipated to an electric tingle and then to nothing, but not normalcy. A few minutes later, Abe found he could stand. With his breathing eased, he inhaled and exhaled deeply, regularly, through his nostrils. Then Abe wiped the sticky spittle from the corner of his mouth and decided some things. He would call Ira later this afternoon. He would begin writing the Carnival Barker show, for himself or for someone else, tomorrow. And he would keep his appointment with the doctor today.

Abe stood under the awning of his apartment building while the doorman hailed a cab. His gut throbbed with fear. The only thing worse than going to the doctor when you didn't have to was going when you did. Standing with his left leg braced against a tall, terra cotta pot, Abe wondered why the false reports of his death had never really bothered him. Maybe he had always known that death, when it finally came, would be all too real.

LOOK AND FEEL

In high school, I hung out with the heavy-metal kids. Before first bell, we would gather around a table in the cafeteria to trade tapes—an Iron Maiden bootleg for a Megadeth EP, Slayer demos for some Swedish death metal. I didn't like the music much, but I liked drawing the way it made me feel. While my sort-of friends banged their heads over air guitars, I drew thunderheads and snarling dogs and broken limbs in pen. When a drawing was finished, I would make photocopies and hand them out to the rest of the guys, who would tape them to bathroom walls and locker doors and the covers of their chemistry textbooks.

By the end of my freshman year of college, I was done with metal and done with drawing, except when my graphic-design classwork demanded a quick sketch. What I wanted was to be in a band. All my friends were either members or fans of Simon Eyes, a band of indie kids a year ahead of me at school. I went to every Simon Eyes show. I watched them rehearse in the unfinished basement of their rotting bungalow. And, in the privacy of my off-campus apartment,

I taught myself to play their melodic, privileged-kid punk on electric guitar. Then I waited. When the band's second guitarist, Jimmy, went down with strep throat two days before a Saturday gig, I could have said honestly that I hadn't wished that particular illness on him, as I'd pinned my hopes on either mono or flu.

While Jimmy slept on the second floor, I joined the rest of Simon Eyes in the basement. We started with "Messy," the band's usual opener. I felt myself struggling to keep up—I had never played the song at full speed—but managed to get through it without missing a single chord. And, to my relief, I sang the backing vocals on key, though I doubt if anyone heard me, as I wouldn't put my mouth within a foot of Jimmy's microphone. I wanted to be a part of Simon Eyes, but not enough to risk getting strep.

After "Messy," the lead guitarist led us into an up-tempo charger called "Kick It." Again, I played all the right chords at all the right times. But nothing I played on either song had sounded quite right. The band heard something missing, too. They offered to let me borrow Jimmy's guitar. I declined. So they ran my guitar through an effects pedal and we tried another song. This time, I worried less about the notes and tried to play with greater energy, bobbing my head in double time and punctuating a few downstrokes with an exaggerated follow-through. But something about my playing was still cold. After the third song, the guys thanked me for trying. I unplugged and went home. Simon Eyes played their show that Saturday without Jimmy and without me. To my ears, they didn't miss either one of us.

Back in my apartment after the show, I stood in my kitchenette listening to the music in my head and the ringing in my ears. Then I pulled a clean sheet of paper from the tray of my printer, grabbed a pen from the mug on the counter, and sat down at the tiny kitchen table. The first thing I drew was a jagged line—a distant, rocky landscape—across the width of the page, about two inches up from the bottom. An inch or so above the horizon, I sketched a series of short arcs that overlapped at their tips, and continued in a counterclockwise progression until I had made a circle. Then I shaded in part of the circle's bottom-right quadrant until it read as a nearly centered sphere. When I leaned back in my chair and saw the whole page, I realized that I had drawn how Simon Eyes' music made me feel.

A moment later I was stooped over the page again, holding my pen above a rock formation on the horizon line and envisioning a second sphere, smaller and farther away than the first with just the hint of a fissure at the top, a new wound or old damage nearly healed. Then I put down my pen and got up from the table without sketching another stroke. The second sphere didn't belong on that page. Whatever it was—cold planet, maybe, or battered moon—it wasn't part of how Simon Eyes' music made me feel. It was me.

I met Nell at Simon Eyes' final show. A year later, I followed her to Chicago. We lived together in a three-room apartment in Ukrainian Village. I found freelance work designing websites for IT consultants and trade-show booths for software vendors. At night I went to shows at small clubs, sometimes with Nell, sometimes without her. I gave every band—even the openers—two songs to make me feel something. If they didn't, I would spend the rest of their set in front of whatever wall the venue had designated for promotion of upcoming shows. Many of the posters on the wall were little more than flyers, sloppily copied pen-and-ink illustrations like the ones I had done in high school. Others wrinkled where printer ink had saturated the cheap paper or bore white stripes where dying ink-jet cartridges had passed but failed to cover. But at least one poster on every wall was different. It was usually bigger than the rest, the paper thick and textured, the colors rich and raised, like oil paint on a canvas. And whether a polygonal abstraction or a faithful rendering of the human form, the best of these screen-printed images seemed to capture something—though I couldn't have said what—about the music of the bands they promoted.

After months of evenings spent staring at posters, I started saving every dollar that wasn't earmarked for food, rent or show tickets so that I could buy time in a small screen-printing studio in an old warehouse just north of the housing projects. Two fluorescent tubes buzzed in an aluminum fixture that hung by two thin, rusted chains from the high plank ceiling. Plaster chips crunched underfoot with every step, and two open bags of lye were slumped in the corner by the fire door. But from ten in the morning until four in the afternoon, Monday through Friday, the studio and all of its printing accoutrements—a reusable polyester screen, a hose to wash it out, a transparency copier, an ultraviolet light box, a squeegee and an old manual press—were mine to use.

That first morning, I disinfected the place, as I didn't know who else used the studio, if they washed their hands after using the bathroom down the wide hallway or sneezed without covering their mouths. I sprayed Formula 409 on the squeegee grip, the hose nozzle, the face of the old, paint-splattered CD player, the wooden frame of the screen, and the heads of the screws that locked the screen to the press, wiping each surface with a clean paper towel. When I was finished, plaster still powdered the floor and lye dust floated in the air, but my chances of catching so much as a cold were basically nil.

Before leaving, I picked a tattered issue of *Vanity Fair* off the floor—the even layer of dust on the cover proved it hadn't been touched in months—and placed it on the press. This would become a daily practice. If I returned the next morning to find the magazine in even a slightly different position, I disinfected everything I thought I might touch.

My first few experiments in the studio were failures. I would make a bad stencil, or use the wrong kind of ink, or add a second color while the first was still wet. But eventually I got comfortable with the process and the equipment, and the results grew more accomplished even as the experiments grew more complex.

One day, I brought the best of these studies, a side-angle perspective of a Chinese checkerboard, home to Nell. She ran her fingers lightly over the ink, smiled without parting her lips, and hung the poster on our refrigerator using magnets that promoted teams we'd never cheered for and tradesmen we'd never hired.

The next morning I went into the studio, opened a copy of the *Chicago Reader* on the rickety wooden drafting table, and scanned the list of upcoming shows. Most of the names I recognized were those of nu-metal acts playing arenas or classic rockers charging eighty-five dollars a ticket at more intimate venues. Those bands might have needed promotion, but they weren't going to get it from me. Then I saw that the Chamber Strings, a Chicago band better loved outside Chicago and a favorite of Nell's, were scheduled to play the Metro in six days. Eight-dollar tickets were still available. While making dinner two nights before, Nell and I had listened to an album of the band's lush, jangly pop—doubled melodies and layered harmonies laid over a harpsichord and twelve-string electric guitars. The triumph I felt in their major choruses was undercut by minor bridges that made me yearn for something I couldn't name. I didn't fully understand those feelings, but I knew I could draw them.

The central image was a frisbee, fire engine red and lozenge-shaped against a pale blue sky. Thin black arcs indicated the direction of the frisbee's flight, and suggested it would elude the spread-eagle cartoon in the paper's lower-left quadrant. The sleeve of an orange, cable-knit sweater descended from the hand to the bottom edge of the page. Each word in the band's name was given its own line at the top, brown letterforms stacked in neat but imperfect columns. Written in small, black caps, the venue, date, time and ticket price fit comfortably on a single line below the band's name, leaving a few inches of clear blue sky above the frisbee.

I made thirty prints, ruining only four in the process. When they had dried, I signed the twenty-six survivors with a mechanical pencil and laid each one flat in an old nylon portfolio. Then I posted them in the usual places: Reckless Records (both locations), Laurie's Planet of Sound, the concrete kiosks in Roscoe Village. At the end of each stop, I coated my hands and my stapler with hand sanitizer to keep the infectious filth of Chicago's walls and door handles outside my car.

I also brought a print to the Metro. The tired-looking girl behind the tempered glass of the ticket window picked up the phone, dialed four numbers, said something I couldn't hear, and hung up. "Wait over there," she said, pointing in the direction of the club's main doors.

A few minutes later, an older guy wearing a black t-shirt, black jeans, and a gold chain opened one of the black metal doors. "You've got a poster?"

"Yeah," I said.

I held the print out to the side like a bullfighter's cape. When I looked up, the man was nodding just slightly.

"Who hired you?" he said.

"Nobody."

"You with the Chamber Strings?"

"No."

The man looked at me, working his tongue over a tooth in the back of his mouth. Then he pushed the door further open and made room for me to pass. "Straight up the stairs. Staples only. Don't cover any other posters."

With four prints left in my portfolio and two hours before Nell was due home from work, I drove in the general direction of our apartment, keeping an eye out for stores and walls I'd either never seen or failed to consider. I posted one of the remaining prints on the edge of a crowded bulletin board in a Lincoln Square bookstore, and another between a yoga-studio flyer and a farmers-market announcement on a kiosk in North Center. When it started to drizzle, I took to side streets to avoid rush-hour traffic, figuring I had done enough of what I had set out to do.

Driving under a viaduct in Bucktown, I saw something that made me stop. I shifted into park, turned on my hazards, and walked around the front of the car to get a closer look at the viaduct's cinderblock wall. The masonry beneath the mineral-stained steel was new, and the even coat of eggshell paint still had its gloss. Rainwater, seeping through from the railroad tracks above, rolled down the wall in beads.

I opened my trunk, grabbed a roll of duct tape and tore off five strips. I folded the strips into double-sided adhesive pads and stuck them to the backside of a print, putting one in each corner and one in the middle. Then I pressed the frisbee and the tape pad behind it to the wall, straightened the print on its adhesive axis, and smoothed it into place with slow forearm sweeps from the center to the corners. When the print was right where I wanted it, I sealed the four edges with duct tape.

With exhaust fumes blowing on my calves, I stood behind the car and beheld the poster, framed in gray against a luxurious expanse of white. I couldn't be sure that anyone would pass by before the Chamber Strings played their show or railroad workers ripped down the print, but I knew that whoever did would stop. They would read the words and imagine their own narratives about the frisbee and the hand and the sky. In this spot, the poster would compete for fewer pairs of eyes, but it seemed to stand a better chance of winning some.

On the way home, I passed other out-of-the-way places where my poster would've seized notice—an alley stairwell lit by a single, grated bulb, and a freshly poured sidewalk—but I wanted to save the final print for Nell.

When I heard a key grind into the lock I was at the kitchen sink washing my hands in water as hot as I could stand.

"Hey," Nell said, closing the door behind her.

"Hey," I answered.

Nell stepped out of her high heels, kicked them behind the door, and set her tote on the kitchen counter. She hugged me from the side as I dried my hands and arms with paper towels. Then I turned to face her and held the side of her head to my chest. Her hair smelled clean.

Suddenly Nell's hands dropped from around my waist. She stood up straight, looking over the counter into our living room.

"What's wrong?" I asked.

She stepped out of my loosened embrace, walked around the counter and stood over the small table where I had laid out the last print for her. A few strands of her straight hair dangled in front of her face. "Where'd you get this?" she asked.

I laughed. "I made it."

Nell kept her eyes on the poster for another moment. Then she retraced her steps over the hardwood and the tile, laid her arms on my shoulders and clasped her hands behind my neck. "It's really, really good."

As Nell raised herself on tiptoe and brought her face closer to mine, I recalled that she had awoken that morning with a sore throat. I was also sure that the shredded remnants of whatever she had eaten for lunch were decaying between her teeth. But I didn't care—nothing had ever stopped me from kissing Nell.

After we had our kiss, she nuzzled the crown of her

head into my neck and squeezed me as tightly as she could. Then she stepped back and hopped in long sidesteps toward our hand-me-down, off-white leather couch, smiling like a little girl expecting to be chased. "So are we going to the show?"

The way in which she'd asked made it clear that she thought she already knew the answer was "yes." But my smile flattened as I realized I had no intention of attending the Chamber Strings' performance. I believed my poster had captured the way I would feel at that show, in the presence of the band's music. And if I was wrong, I didn't want to know.

A week later, I received a one-line e-mail at the address posted on my website. "If you made the Chamber Strings poster with the frisbee on it," the e-mail read, "write back." I did, and the note's author, a local promoter named Jon Dacus, commissioned an original poster—and 100 prints—to publicize an upcoming appearance by the Leonids, a UK band that had been a favorite of mine at the time of its breakup three years before. I wrote back again to say that I would take the job and asked Dacus how he'd gotten my name. "You scribbled it on your prints," he responded. "Promote my show better than you promote yourself."

The Leonids were scheduled to play in two weeks at the Double Door, an asymmetrical room with a long bar and a capacity of three hundred—five hundred if you counted the basement, which was outfitted with pool tables and wall-mounted TVs tuned to a closed-circuit feed of the stage. I had attended many shows at the Double Door since moving to Chicago, but none since I went to see Rancid.

I was third in line when the doors opened, ensuring a place at the front of the stage and, if I stayed put, an unobstructed view of the headliners. The opening act was a teenage skatecore band from the Bay Area. They were not good. But I didn't turn my back on them or stare at the floor. I pointed my eyes at the stage and waited them out, clapping a little at the end of every song. I was paying enough attention to tell that the lead singer didn't look well. I had seen unwell lead singers before, but, until that moment, I had never seen a guy vomit during a set. The candy-pink liquid hit the front edge of the stage and splashed onto my neck and into my mouth, which was twisted open in disgust. Then I threw up, further scattering my fellow Rancid die-hards.

Since then, many bands I had been desperate to see had played the Double Door, but I could hardly think of the place without gagging. I consoled myself with the notion that I would never have to learn that the Leonids' live show evoked different feelings in me than the ones I captured in my poster.

The Leonids had made their name blending wry, literate lyrics about London's drug culture with dirty drums and major-key hooks, but everything I had read about the album they had reunited to record warned fans not to expect any stompers, leaving me with little idea of what to expect. With U.S. release of the album still a week away, I bought an imported copy and drove straight to my studio.

The CD player occupied its usual spot on the floor across from the drafting table. The issue of *Vanity Fair* lay face down in the dust alongside it. I disinfected the screen, the squeegee, the hose nozzle, the press, and the player itself.

Then I put the Leonids disc in the player and pressed play.

Track one opened with a distant, muffled piano chord that nearly receded into the background crackle before the next chord sounded. A third chord followed more closely. This progression of three chords, each shrouded in fuzz, continued for three more measures. During the fifth measure, a finger-picked acoustic guitar joined the piano, complementing and connecting the chords. Then the Leonids' two lead vocalists entered the mix, echoing over the instrumentation in cigarette-strained harmony, accompanied on the low end by the steady hum of an electronic bass note.

On their first two albums, the Leonids had treated each song like an opportunity that they took pleasure in wasting, and that wastefulness had been part of their appeal. Now, as I leaned against the press listening to their new album, the Leonids sounded utterly different. Yes, the distorted guitars had been quieted and the drums replaced with brushed, airy percussion, but the differences ran deeper than mere instrumentation. Songs built to resolutions where they had once petered out. Words were being sung, not sneered, and instruments were being played instead of pounded. The Leonids' were trying, and their efforts seemed infused with an almost grateful reverence, as if they appreciated these songs and the chance they had been given to make them.

That reverence infected me. I started sketching while the seventh track played at my back. When I stepped back from the drafting table, the album was over, and on the page was an overhead perspective of a newborn being laid in a crib. The eyes on her scrunched little face were shut tight, as if she were having a bad dream. An inch of shadow outlined the left side of her body. Her head was supported by a man's left hand. His right hand cradled her puffy, diapered rear. The crib's fitted sheet, patterned with tiny fleurs de lis, was visible above the baby's head and in patches between the arms and legs. The ten letters of the band's name, illustrated in three-inch, outline type, were evenly spaced across the top of the page. The date, time, venue and ticket price ran across the bottom in thin, inch-high characters.

As I coated each print with the buttery yellow I had chosen for the fitted sheet, good feeling flowed beneath my concentration. I was getting this right, capturing in image and color the reverent care with which the Leonids now made their music. I almost didn't mind that I wouldn't make it inside the Double Door to feel that reverence again. But as I poured a spreading line of burgundy ink to fill the outlines of the band name and the fleurs de lis, I realized that my endgame for the poster had changed. Now, more than wanting to capture on paper the feelings I would experience if I went to the show, I wanted others to experience what *they* would feel, to know by looking at the poster how the Leonids' music would move or exhilarate or annoy them. Though I hadn't known it then, the best screen-printed posters—the ones I had stared at while bands clamored on stage for my attention—had done that very thing for me. And as I pulled the squeegee down the screen, forcing ink through its unfilled holes, the measuring stick for my success moved outside of myself, and my good feeling followed it.

As soon as I had finished the prints, I rushed home to Nell. When I opened the door, she was shaking a colander over the kitchen sink, turning her head away from the rising steam. Without a word, I knelt on the wood floor alongside the table, unzipped my portfolio, slid my palms under one of the four extra prints I'd made and lifted it onto the table.

Nell poured spaghetti from the colander into a stainless steel pot on the gas range. "Hi," she said, finally.

"Hey," I said. "Can you take a look at this?"

Nell set the colander in the sink and walked around the counter. Supporting herself on the arms of a wooden chair, she leaned forward over the table, as if trying to see what the print would look like posted at eye level on a wall. Her hair hid her face from me.

Though Nell was smiling when she stood up, she looked stricken. "It's amazing, Ted."

I knew there was more. I waited for it.

"It's the strangest poster I've ever seen."

"It makes you feel strange?"

Nell's smile shrank away. "What?"

"How does it make you feel?" I asked.

Nell turned back to the print. "Scared."

Of course Nell was scared—her boyfriend had illustrated a life-like image of a baby, made color prints, and brought one home just for her. I took the back of her neck in my hand—she was trembling a little—and as I kissed her cheek through her hair with my smiling lips, I was sure that the Leonids' cold, haunting soundscapes would scare Nell just as much as my poster had.

The next day, I drove to Jon Dacus' office with 100 prints of the Leonids poster in my portfolio. I climbed three flights of steel stairs, pulled open a heavy fire door, and walked into the timber loft occupied by InMotion Promotion. The receptionist's desk was unattended. A floor-to-ceiling steel lattice held nine plates of frosted glass, blocking sight lines into what I imagined to be the main office. Behind the partition, a desk chair creaked and a woman argued on the telephone. A song I didn't recognize—all shouted vocals and distorted electric guitars—played in the background.

On the wall to the right of the fire door, framed-and-matted pairings of a poster and an untorn ticket hung on a white wall at even intervals and various heights. Each pairing featured an InMotion Promotion show played by a revered band at the moment considered, in hindsight, to be the apex of its artistic achievement: Pavement at the Empty Bottle in '91. Guided By Voices at Lounge Ax in '94. Neutral Milk Hotel at the Elbo Room in '96. All the posters had been professionally produced, but only the Pavement poster had been screen-printed. Its central image—a hand crank beneath the grill of an early automobile—struck me as the perfect visual equivalent of Pavement's grinding guitar sound.

I was still standing in front of the Pavement poster when two guys emerged from behind the steel and glass and made straight for the door. They looked to be about twenty years old. The one in the lead wore a faded green military cap, a red t-shirt, and long, black cargo shorts. The second kid shuffled along behind him, a sweatshirt hood pulled over his head, the right leg of his jeans cuffed to the knee. The black, cylindrical poster cases strapped across their backs like broadswords made the portfolio dangling from my fingers seem more than a little precious.

As the metal door swung shut behind them, a sneaker sole squeaked and a young woman with a helmet of ink-black hair stepped behind the reception desk.

"Hi," she said.

"Hi. I'm here to drop off some prints for Jon Dacus."

The receptionist pointed to a door at the far end of the white wall. "You can lay them on the table in there."

I entered what appeared to be a conference room and laid my portfolio on a long, steel table. I unzipped the portfolio, pulled the stack of prints onto the table and tidied the stack between my hands. Then I stood behind the table, waiting for Jon Dacus to walk in and review my work.

As I waited, I began to worry that, when Dacus saw the baby, he would accuse me of trying to sabotage his ticket sales. I imagined myself saying them out loud and realized that my reasons for drawing and printing this image—and my hopes for what it would evoke in the viewer—might fail to move a concert promoter.

After what had to be ten minutes, Jon Dacus still hadn't shown. No one had. Then it occurred to me that the receptionist hadn't said anything resembling, "Mr. Dacus will be with you in a minute," and that she was probably wondering what the hell I was doing. I flipped my empty portfolio closed and carried it out of the conference room. The receptionist, seated at her desk, darted her eyes at me before returning them to her computer monitor.

As I reached the metal door, I decided to make sure I wasn't walking out on a meeting or leaving my payment in the outbox. "So," I said to the receptionist, "is that it?"

"Yep," she said.

I nodded. "Do you want me to take some of the prints and post them around?"

The receptionist appeared to choke on something—a laugh, maybe? "We do that," she said.

Driving home from the studio two days later, I stopped at a red light on Chicago Avenue and saw three of my Leonids prints on a plywood fence in front of a gutted Ukrainian social club. Across two lanes of traffic and in the shadow of scaffolding that climbed the old building's façade, the yellow of the crib sheets was dulled and the typography nearly invisible, but the babies glowed a grotesque pink. I watched passersby hustle to catch their buses and scanned faces in other stopped cars. So far as I could tell, the prints caught no one's notice but mine.

Two blocks east, I saw one of my prints in the window of a coffee shop and another on the door of a clothing boutique. The idea that there were ninety-five more prints out there kept me driving. I found one taped to the door of the Reckless Records on Broadway and another staple-gunned to the boarded-up window of a former Goldblatt's. Four more were posted on kiosks in North Center and Roscoe Village. Over the next two-and-a-half hours, I spotted thirty-eight prints of my Leonids poster.

The sky was warning-cone orange as I drove toward home, still scanning storefronts for my prints. At Damen and Cortland, I realized I was only blocks from the viaduct under which I'd taped my Chamber Strings poster.

I turned east onto a one-way street, then south again at the first stop sign. The print was still there. I coasted past it, then made a slow U-turn and parked in front of a newly constructed three-flat on the opposite side of the street.

I got out of the car and walked to the nearest of the viaduct's center supports, first taking a side-angle perspective that seemed more appropriate, given the print's surroundings, than a head-on, gallery view. When my eyes had adjusted to the relative darkness beneath the bridge, I saw that the inks, shielded from direct sunlight, had held their color, but that a drop of water had cut a narrow track across the pale blue sky. The marring read like a battle scar. I tried to make a memory of the print as it appeared in that moment, feeling certain that the next time I drove under the viaduct, it would be gone.

When the lights on the bridge's underside flickered on, illuminating the sidewalks and bleeding color from the print with their yellowish tint, I headed for my car. As I reached the driver-side door, a bicycle bell rang twice and a girl laughed. I turned my head to find two guys and a girl pedaling toward the viaduct from the far side. Instinctively, I crept around the back of my car to the passenger side and peered over the hood, waiting for the cyclists to pass. But they didn't. Instead, the young woman, sitting upright on her vintage black cruiser, ramped smoothly up to the sidewalk where it met the street while the guys, one after the other, popped their fat road tires over the curb beneath the viaduct.

I recognized them in pieces: the cylindrical poster cases first, then the military hat and the sweatshirt hood, then the ink-black hair. While the girl I now recognized as Jon Dacus' receptionist looked on, the kid in the military hat opened the case slung across his hooded friend's back and slid out a roll of posters, taking care not to catch any corners on the lip or the lid. He peeled one print off the top, handed it to the receptionist, then re-rolled the curling stack into a tight, even tube, threaded it back into the case, and pressed the lid into place.

I ape-walked to the back of my car and put one knee on the street's graying asphalt. When I looked up again, the kid in the hat was rolling the print art-side out. Then he held the rolled paper in front of the receptionist, who pinned it between the tips of her fingers and thumbs at the print's uninked edges. They were training the paper to lay flat again. The kid in the hood watched them, shifting his weight from one leg to the other, his hands buried in the front pocket of his sweatshirt.

The kid in the hat retrieved the roll of duct tape hanging over his handlebars. After tearing off a half-dozen strips, he folded them into adhesive pads and stuck them to the viaduct wall to the right of my Chamber Strings poster. When he reclaimed the print from the receptionist and unfurled it, I saw the pink baby and the yellow sheets and felt adrenaline pour into my stomach. The kid in the hat lined up the Leonids print alongside the Chamber Strings print, but a little lower, like the silver-medal platform on an Olympic podium, and the receptionist smoothed it against the tape. Then the kid in the hat took the tape roll and framed my Leonids print in gray vinyl.

When they stood back to admire their work, I admired it, too—no wrinkles, no bulges, no waves. Suddenly I was certain that the kid in the hat had found my Chamber Strings print in this place, deciphered my scribbled signature, and fed my name to Dacus. But I would've traded those certainties for some hint that the kid had seen the Chamber Strings play, and that their music had made him feel the same way my poster had.

The hooded kid collapsed on the sidewalk in a comic show of exhaustion. The receptionist laughed and sat down alongside him. The kid in the hat put a new layer of tape around the Chamber Strings print, then lowered himself to the ground. The three of them sat in a half-circle, ribbing the kid in the hood about something—I couldn't tell what. Then the kid in the hat pointed at something in the Leonids print, aiming his arm like the barrel of a gun. The hooded kid pointed at something else, or maybe the same thing. After that, they just sat on the sidewalk and stared at the poster. I stared with them. Leached of her pinkness by the yellow light, the baby looked even more human. The print had never looked as good as it did through their eyes.

Then, without moving his eyes from the poster, the kid in the hood uncovered his head, revealing a sweaty shock of bleached-blond hair. I can't say for sure why he pulled down his hood in that moment. It's possible he wanted to see his friends in his peripheral vision, or to be cooled by the light evening breeze. But that small action—I'm not even sure his friends saw it—changed everything for me. I saw then that the kids weren't just looking at the poster—they had been looking at it all day. Now that the poster wasn't a job, now that they had hung it in a space that they had made their own, they were feeling the reverence I had captured in its image.

I stayed behind my car until they got on their bikes and rode off in the direction from which they had come. They said no words I could hear, though I heard the bicycle bell ring once more after they had pedaled out of sight. I got to my feet, stooped to rub the burn out of the skin beneath my kneecap, and stood in front of my trunk, unable or unwilling to move. The orange in the sky had retreated, and the steady rush of car tires carried from the interstate to my ears. As I listened to the white noise that passes for silence in the city, one thought stated and restated itself in my mind: Nell isn't my only measuring stick anymore. But unlike Nell, these kids wouldn't come home to me after the show and let me grill them about what they had felt. I would have to see for myself if the Leonids made them feel the same reverence that my poster had. And to do that, I would have to go to the Double Door.

That realization quickly became a decision. I was going to the Double Door. I imagined crossing the threshold into the humid darkness of the entryway and handing over my ticket to be torn, then rounding a corner and catching a glimpse of the stage.

Then I leaned over the curb and emptied my stomach into the gutter.

In the days leading up to the show, I waged a misinformation campaign against the Leonids' opening act. "They're pianists," I told Nell. "Two uprights on stage, facing each other. *The Reader* called them 'the Fabulous Baker Boys of indie rock.'" All lies, but they kept me away from the Double Door until five minutes before the Leonids were scheduled to take the stage.

Standing in line behind Nell, I fought my fear with reason. I knew the Double Door to be, relatively speaking, a clean place—the glassware had always passed my inspections, and I had a distinct memory of inhaling the fumes of a harsh disinfectant in the bathroom. More importantly, I figured that no one on stage or in the crowd was more likely to vomit that night than I was.

I held my breath as I handed my ID to the bouncer and

took it back. Exhaling through pursed lips, I turned my ticket over to the doorman and accepted a stub in return. When I had cleared those hurdles without incident, I flushed with excitement, and even a little pride. Then it occurred to me that, in the last twenty seconds, I had indirectly touched the hands of every person in the club. That thought, in the closeness of the entryway, was enough to turn my stomach. But I pulled a bottle of hand sanitizer from my pocket, squeezed the clear gel into my left palm, and spread it over my hands, fighting off, for the moment, the mental and bacterial threats to my well being. I followed Nell down the entryway onto the club's main floor. When I realized that she was headed for the front of the stage, I touched her forearm. She turned around to face me.

"I'm going to watch from the bar," I said.

"OK," she said. "I'll find you."

I went to the bar and ordered a ginger ale—just in case. I took a sip of my drink and scanned the crowd. Nell had worked her way to a spot in front, between the two singers' microphones. Behind her, a tall guy with sunglasses and messy hair was shouting into the ear of a guy who had a Union Jack wrapped around his shoulders. Further back, on an open, elevated island, the soundman had his head down, checking the settings of his faders and knobs against whatever was written on the wrinkled white sheet he held under the light on his console. I had started panning back toward the front when I saw Dacus's receptionist standing near the stairs that led down to the basement pool hall. The sleeves of her small black t-shirt barely covered her shoulders, leaving her long, thin arms exposed. She crossed them and shifted her weight—I imagined she was looking impatient and unkind so that no one would try to talk to her. Eventually, the kid in the hat emerged at the top of the stairs, followed by his bleach-blond buddy, whose hood hung limply between his shoulder blades. My relief at seeing them was followed immediately by a twinge in my stomach, more nerves than nausea. My audience was fully assembled now.

When the house lights went out a few minutes later, the crowd cheered, and the Leonids—the two guitarist/singers, a drummer, a bassist, and a keyboard player—took the stage. The drummer settled onto his stool and, just as the crowd had begun to quiet down, counted off the first four beats of the opener. With their eyes on the drummer and their backs to the crowd, the two guitarists came in on the fifth beat with exaggerated downstokes that sent a loud, distorted chord careening into the audience. That chord was followed by another, just as chunky, just as loud. The song was not from the Leonids' new album—it was the third song on their second album, and they were playing it live the same way they had recorded it. The musicianship was sloppy. The vocals dripped with contempt. The Leonids had no reverence about them.

In front of me, silhouetted heads bounced with the four beats of each measure. Nell's hair hugged the side of her head as she jumped, and mushroomed out in strands as she descended. The poster kids stood their ground at the top of the stairs, unmoving and unmoved.

The second song—track five of the Leonids' debut—was all sneers and leers and kiss-offs. Where was the music from the new album? Had reviews of the album been that bad? Had audiences in New York or Detroit stripped the Leonids of their nerve? The answers, I decided, didn't matter. Nell, still bouncing, wasn't scared. And by the first chorus of the fourth song—another stomper—the poster kids were nowhere to be found. I propped my forearms on the bar and hung my head over them, absorbing the crashing treble and thumping bass with my back.

The fourth song ended with a cymbal crash, and the audience erupted on cue. As the applause died out, a low, synthesized note spread through the room. I felt it in my feet and in my chest more than I heard it. Conversation thickened behind me as Leonids fans, who must have taken the drone for some kind of intermission, packed around the bar to order drinks.

When the first note was replaced by a second—this one a little higher, something more like music—the vibrations in my body weakened. I turned around and stood on my toes just as the drummer began tracing circles on the snare drum and ride cymbal with his brushes, creating a steady, airy rush, like a long exhalation. The two guitarists stood with their instruments hanging from their necks and their heads bowed. One of them twisted just slightly at the waist, catching and releasing the stage light with his guitar's chrome tuning pegs.

When I broke through the crowd at the bar, the audience was only four-deep at the stage. Inexplicably, two kids were still pogoing up and down. But Nell's silhouette was still. Keeping his left hand on the bass note, the keyboard player reached his right hand to another deck and played a fuzzy piano chord. He held it, then let it fade and pressed out two more in succession. The other guitarist picked the notes of a barre chord from top to bottom and back to the middle, then changed the shape of his left hand and played a new chord with the same picking pattern. Finally, in smooth unison, the two singers stepped forward, touched their lips to microphones, and sang softly in reverberant harmony. The bassist joined with a single, low note. At the start of the next measure, he played it again. The sound was vast and barren, but it lacked nothing. The Leonids, for the first time that night, sounded unbroken.

I looked to the stairs. The poster kids weren't there. But as I turned back to the stage, I saw them standing about twenty feet away from me in the diminished crowd. The blond kid, his hood down, stood between the receptionist and the kid in the hat. People passed behind and in front of them on their way to the bar and the bathrooms, but the poster kids were undistracted—they kept their eyes on the stage and their bodies square to its front edge. They were feeling, at last, what my poster had promised they'd feel.

As the Leonids built to the song's low peak with a gently ascending bass line and a wash of distorted guitar, I moved closer to the stage, brushing past the shoulders of rapt onlookers until I had squeezed into a place at the front, to the left of the two singers. Their eyes were squeezed shut now, and I imagined for a moment that the Leonids, too, experienced music as feeling and feeling as image, and that they were giving themselves over to the pictures in their heads.

I held my hand out over the stage. The intermittent thump of the kick drum jumped from the sagging wood to my palm like electric current. The black paint beneath my hand had faded to a shade of gray, and it occurred to me that I was standing almost exactly where I'd stood when the punk singer's vomit had splashed on and into me. But

I didn't care. I closed my eyes and laid my hand flat on the stage, living out my new oneness with the Leonids in the only way I could.

When the song ended, I opened my eyes. Everyone around the stage was clapping except for Nell. Her arms hung at her sides as she stared at me, her lips parted just barely. And my first thought was that my poster had kept its promise to her, too. She was scared now.

POSTGAME

I was a three-point specialist, but my hands were what kept me in the game. Bigger players were able to push me around, and smaller guys could beat me off the dribble, but I was able to hold my own by tipping passes, disrupting crossovers, even blocking a shot every now and then.

Reporters and commentators had noted my "quick hands" for years. But a few months into my twelfth season, a *Chicago Sun-Times* columnist described my hands as "smart." He meant the remark as a compliment, but that wasn't how I saw it—smart hands knew what to do, but they weren't quick enough to do it anymore.

A week after Chicago's exit from the playoffs, my agent, Perry, called to tell me that the team would not be reupping my contract, and that he would make the rounds to find out who could use me. By this time, Perry had negotiated twelve one-year contracts on my behalf. I knew there wasn't anyone better able to convince a GM that he needed a player like me, and that I was the only player like me available.

With no contract, I went home to Iowa City and to Liz.

For most of my career, she had enjoyed watching me earn a living playing the game I loved. But for the last few seasons, Liz seemed to be enduring each game, happy only when it had been checked off the list of things to get through before she could have the family that she'd always wanted and that I'd agreed to start when my playing days were over. She was still outwardly supportive, sitting with me when the phone wasn't ringing and celebrating with me when, at last, I signed with someone, but I knew she had spent the last few summers hoping that Perry would come up empty.

I woke up at five-thirty every morning to lift weights, run sprints, and take a thousand shots, including four hundred three-pointers. If I started my workout any later in the day, some other activity—grocery shopping or TV watching—would get the best of my energy. Perry would call every few days to report that he had an iron in the fire—a chance to replace an injured sharpshooter in Portland, or provide a veteran defensive presence in Atlanta—but as July came to an end, he still hadn't gotten me an offer.

I would arrive home from the gym to find new little touches around the house: a flowering plant on the kitchen countertop, insulated shades in the bedroom next to ours, a circular mahogany coffee table in place of the glass one we had bought only two years before. As I sat at the kitchen table nursing a Gatorade in my t-shirt and tearaways, my exhausted legs splayed out across the ceramic-tiled floor, Liz would emerge from some corner of the house.

"How was the workout?" she would ask, rubbing my neck and shoulders.

"Fine."

"Did you hear anything from Perry?"

"Not yet."

She would squeeze me once more, as hard as she could, then kiss my head through sweaty hair and go back to whatever she had been doing when I got home.

I kept up my workouts through training camp and the preseason. When the regular season began, I watched games on television, trying to figure where I might fit on a given team, hoping to find holes only I could fill and weaknesses only I could shore up. Occasionally I found one or the other, but the best I could do was mention it to Perry in a sort of offhand way, and when I did, I often found that he had already tried that tack. "I'll check again, though," he would say. "Maybe something's changed."

When I found myself hoping that every guard who fell to the floor had torn a ligament or broken a bone, I would turn off the TV and go to bed, steeling myself to wake up and work out the next morning.

The regular season was nearly a month old when I watched all forty-eight minutes of a Chicago road win over Houston. I hardly moved a muscle during the game, but my heart was beating as if I were on the floor with those guys, all but two of whom I had played with the previous season. When the game was over, I sat in my plush leather chair, waiting for my heartbeat to return to normal. Then, for the first time since the night of that final playoff loss in Chicago, I went to bed without setting an alarm.

The next day, Perry told me to announce my retirement.

"It's a reminder you're still out there," he said. "When

we were shopping you in the off-season, none of these guys had a need. But now, some of their teams are below .500, shooting twenty-five percent from behind the arc, and failing to give a shit on defense. Somebody might see the release and figure he can get you on the cheap to fix those problems."

I didn't believe I was out of the league because the best basketball minds in the world—men who spent every waking moment looking for any angle that would help their teams win more games—had forgotten I existed. But the possibility—remote as it was—that a smudgy fax with my name on it would be handed to just the right guy at the right time had value in itself. It gave me a reason to set my alarm.

"Fine. Write it and send it."

"Do you want to see it?"

"No."

"What reason do you want to give for retiring?"

I thought about that. "Don't give a reason."

"No reason?"

"No."

"All right," Perry said. "It'll be out this afternoon."

I flipped the phone closed. As I stood in my kitchen, replaying the conversation in my head, I started to wonder how long I could go without a contract offer—two days? a week?—before my retirement was more fact than gambit.

I worked out the next morning, then spent the rest of the day—and the next two—watching Japan Tour Golf. No one called.

On the third day, Liz sat down on the couch and watched with me for a while. During a commercial, she turned to me, tucked her feet in front of her and hugged her left shin. "I went off my birth control," she said.

I looked at her for a moment. "How long ago?"

"Almost a month now."

I nodded, and my eyes rested on the new coffee table for a moment. Then I made myself smile and made it look natural. Liz smiled back, looking relieved to be sharing at last the sense of anticipation she had been hiding. She rocked back and forth on her little haunches, rested her chin on her knee, and looked up at me. "Do you wanna try?"

It took me a moment to understand what she meant. "Now?"

"Why not?" she said, smiling and rocking again.

I knew the right answer and gave it.

Liz sprang to her feet and bounded into the bedroom, taking off her sweatshirt on the way. As I walked after her, I realized I had been foolish to think that time would make my retirement real. Only Liz could do that.

By the time the NBA playoffs were over, Liz was six months pregnant with our son, and I was the face of a camp for promising high-school basketball players. James Macon, an Iowa City entrepreneur, had called me with an offer to buy into his sports-camp business after reading about my retirement in the *Press-Citizen*. He said he wanted to attach "the Tim Vilinski brand," as he put it, to his Hawkeye Hoops Camp. When I had officially signed on, Macon printed new brochures and found beds for fifty additional campers. The two-week session sold out in ten days.

The first morning of camp, the coaches led the young players through a stretching regimen while an Iowa assistant talked my ear off about a new zone defense he had come up with. I could feel the kids looking at me as they stretched, then looking away, then looking back again. I knew what they were thinking: that's him? He doesn't look tall enough or strong enough. Such opinions had dogged me throughout my career, and I had treated every possession as an opportunity to prove them wrong. I didn't know quite what to do with them now.

The coaches ran the campers through their drills. They dribbled around cones, flashed to the basket after setting picks, and shuffled the length of the court with their heads up and their hands out. When I thought it would do some good, I pulled a player aside and tried to help him by changing the position of his guide hand or demonstrating the proper way to front a man in the post. I found myself most eager to help the players who worked the hardest and I knew exactly why: they reminded me of me.

By the middle of the second week of camp, I could feel the kids bucking under the constraints of the drills. They wanted to get in the flow of a game. But even their half-court scrimmages were halted repeatedly by coaches intent on teaching the proper way to move without the ball or defend the pick-and-pop.

At the end of that week, James Macon stood at center court and addressed the boys, who were seated around him on the floor. "You fellas have worked hard these last two weeks," he said. "And it's a good thing you have, because tonight the coaches will be breaking you into teams for tomorrow's round-robin tournament."

Many of the boys clapped at this announcement. Those

who didn't nodded their heads.

"And as you know," Macon continued, "Tim Vilinski will be rotating on and off your rosters, playing at least one game with every team." The clapping was louder this time. One boy even whooped. Standing on the sideline, I kept my eyes on the floor and hoped the heat in my face wasn't turning it red. If playing in the camp tournament was among my partnership obligations, I didn't recall Macon saying so.

That night I went to my file cabinet, looking for the contract I had signed. I found the camp brochure first. Alongside my photo on page three was the carrot that had been dangled in front of the campers: "Play with former NBA guard Tim Vilinski!"

I walked into the sports complex the next morning to find the campers warming up with stone-faced seriousness. Many of them, I noticed, were back to the bad habits we had spent the better part of two weeks trying to correct. I realized then how badly it would have hurt me just to *watch* this tournament. Even if they played the best basketball of their young lives—and even if I played with them—these kids would butcher the game, and my playing would make me party to the travesty. The only way to get through, I decided, was not to play as a player, but to think of these games as teaching opportunities—controlled scrimmages with a little less control. As a player, I would expect nothing less than the best performance I could muster. As a teacher, I would be free to do what referees do—keep up with the ball and try to stay out of the way.

I started that first game at about half speed—teacher speed—facilitating good ball movement and helping teammates who got beat on defense. Though most interested in teaching by example, I gave a few one-sentence seminars on topics like dribbling without a purpose and talking back to the refs. I also reinforced some good habits. On our fourth possession, my team's tiny point guard dribbled into the lane, drew my man to himself, then kicked the ball out to me for an open seventeen-footer. After I knocked down the shot, I pointed to him and said, "Good look." He acknowledged my compliment with a cool nod, as if he set up former NBA guards for jumpers all the time. I smiled.

At about the five-minute mark, our opponents gave up on the perimeter passing the coaches had taught them and reverted to playground tactics, isolating defenders on the wing and trying to beat them to the rim off the dribble. Even at half speed I was able to help defend the basket, changing would-be layups into low-percentage scoops and blocking a couple out of the air. But one kid, a wiry athlete with dark wispy hair on his upper lip, drove the lane and scored over my outstretched arm. When I turned around, he was skipping backwards down the court with his arms hanging limp at his sides, staring at me and shaking his head.

From that moment on I went full speed and all the lessons I taught were wordless. I set picks that would've stood up an NBA power forward. I ran the baseline without mercy, waiting for the young player guarding me to tire then demanding the ball and knocking down whatever shot I had. I even drove right at the kid who had tried to show me up, and when I'd made my layup and sent him sliding across the floor on his backside, I immediately turned and ran back to play defense. I couldn't have put that lesson into words if I had tried.

At the end of the game, I had missed only one shot—my signature baseline three, as it happened—and the portable scoreboard at mid-court read 47 to 17 in our favor. I congratulated my teammates and wished them luck in the next game, which they would play without me. They each touched a fist to mine, but a few of the kids seemed to shy away a bit, as if they were afraid of me or embarrassed, somehow.

As I grabbed a towel from the laundry cart behind the basket, James Macon called my name and waved me over. When we were on the other side of the floor-to-ceiling tarpaulin that divided the camp from women's volleyball practice, Macon said, "What are you doing?"

"What do you mean?"

"You've got to take it easier on these kids."

I nodded, looking over his shoulder at the dozens of volleyballs scattered across the far end of the court.

He leaned into my field of vision. "We understand each other?"

"Yeah," I said, looking at him now.

Macon walked past me and around to the other side of the tarpaulin, where he greeted a camp sponsor. I understood that the majority partner in my business had given me an order, but I didn't know how to follow it.

My next team, wearing red mesh pinnies, won the tip-off, and as I ran down the floor, it occurred to me that I could spend our offensive possessions setting picks—good picks, but not jawbreakers—that would give my young teammates a half-step on their defenders. The first possession, which ended with our point guard running his man into my chest and converting a ten-foot jumper, felt good. The next one felt even better. I was playing hard, I was contributing, but with my wrists crossed at my waist I was managing to keep the ball—and the game—out of my hands.

But leaving defense to the kids didn't work. Repeatedly, players in blue pinnies cut to the basket, leaving my teammates in red scrambling to catch them, too late to do anything but swipe at the air behind the ball. I could have blocked those shots—or made them tougher to take, at least—and every part of me demanded I do exactly that. But I didn't. I stayed with my man and boxed him out from rebounds, but the blue team didn't miss enough shots for my boxing out to matter.

By the ten-minute mark, every defensive possession was a humiliation—and not just for me. My teammates wilted, seeming to realize as they played that if they weren't good enough to win with a former pro, all their hard work had come to nothing. And every bullet pass, every breakaway layup, every fall-away jumper made by a member of the blue team was tainted because I hadn't done all I could to prevent it. The kids in blue should've taken my half-effort as an insult, but they didn't. They seemed somehow immune to everything.

With seven minutes left to play and our team down by seventeen, the blue team's best player, a small forward with a child's energy and a man's body, beat his man off the dribble again. Without thinking, I stepped in front of him as he careened toward the rim, my fists laid one over the other at my groin. His eyes opened wide and then, just before impact, shut tight. I absorbed the blow from his forearm with my chest, and heard my teeth click as his elbow struck my chin like an uppercut. The whistle blew just as I hit the floor.

He might have called the young player for charging, but

the referee, probably a local high-school official earning a little cash on the side, gave the foul to me. I didn't mind. The collision had satisfied something in me, like scratching an itch or emptying my bladder would have done.

The next time down the floor, the young forward drove the lane again. I rushed into his path, knowing I would be called for another foul, and felt the release as his shoulder pressed the air out of my lungs and my right hip hit the floor. I made it to my feet first and extended my hand to him. He made a point of getting up without my help.

The blue team's next possession began with the young forward snapping a rebound out of the air, turning, and dribbling headlong down the center lane. I beat him down the floor and stood in front of the rim, bracing to embrace the impact, and when it came, I felt both pain and satisfaction. This time the foul was called on the kid, and when I looked up from the floor, three of my teammates—proud and unsmiling—offered their hands to help me up. They thought I was doing this for them.

When I was called for my fifth and final foul, our team was down by twenty-seven, with twenty-two seconds remaining. I sat in a folding chair while boys in red pinnies rushed up the court to narrow the margin of our defeat by a meaningless two points. And when the buzzer finally sounded, my first thought was how grateful I was that my son hadn't been born in time to see this.

Before he died, my father made a point of telling me that I would find something worth doing when I was finished playing ball, and that when I had a child of my own, I would love that child from the very beginning. He was half right.

I'm still trying to figure it out, actually. Does a man's brain chemistry or blood pressure change when he holds his child? When I held Matthew, whether he was gurgling, sleeping or crying, I would lower the volume and timbre of my voice without thinking and move with a fluidity I'd never had off the court. And Matthew didn't cry much. When he'd been changed or fed or given his pacifier, he generally quieted down. It gave you the feeling that if he could have asked politely for what he needed, he would have.

I often looked in on him while he slept. Even turned all the way up, those baby monitors don't always pick up the sound of breathing which, to my mind, makes them close to useless. You can hear a baby cry from blocks away. What you need is to hear him breathing.

When I stood at the rail of Matthew's crib, watching his chest rise and fall and feeling his warm breath on the back of my hand, I would have some variation of the same waking dream. Matthew is asleep in his car seat, which has been placed on a table. Suddenly, a projectile—a rock or a baseball or a dumbbell—is fired directly at him from an unseen machine. I rush into the projectile's path and let it hit me. As I get to my feet, another projectile is fired. I manage to block it with my face. Then, peering out through the pain, I get up and wait for the next one.

By the time Matthew was a few months old, I was spending my weekdays at the offices of an old college classmate who had become Iowa City's biggest developer. I sat in on meetings and spoke up when I thought I had something sensible to say, but mostly I shook the hands of old Hawkeye fans with farmland to sell. The work wasn't much, but I could get through it, and when I got home, what I did for a living—or what I didn't do—didn't matter much, even to me. All the same, when the NBA season started up that fall, I didn't watch any games. I felt all right for the first time in a long time and that feeling, I knew by then, was fragile.

When winter's grip on Iowa City began to loosen, I made it my routine to wake up when Matthew did and walk him to the bagel shop in the strip mall a few blocks from our house. We would eat our breakfast—two bagels with cream cheese for me, oatmeal for him. Then I would read the paper in my sweatshirt and tearaways before heading home to change into my new uniform—a golf shirt, khakis and loafers.

That day, Matthew and I were up at about six. As I dressed him, he stared at the long shadows on the pale yellow walls of his bedroom. Except for a few gurgles and grunts he was silent, as if he sensed the morning stillness and was unwilling to disturb it.

But once inside the bagel shop, emboldened by the music and the bright lights and the chatter of cashiers and customers, Matthew spoke up. His sounds weren't words, but he was talking to me, and as I carried our breakfast to our usual booth and stirred the heat out of his oatmeal, I did my best to hold up my end of the conversation.

When we had finished eating, I turned my attention to the sports page, and Matthew, seated in his stroller, began identifying things in the shop. First he pointed his tiny hand at a freestanding display of pre-ground coffee. "Da," he said. He looked at me.

"That's right," I said. "Coffee."

The fountain-drink dispenser, to the right of the coffee display, was next. "Da."

"Uh-huh. Pop machine."

Matthew scanned the shop for another interesting object, and I returned my eyes to the paper. The first words I saw were my first and last names. I tried to absorb the surrounding words all at once—I saw "San Antonio" and "retired" and "playoffs." I took a second to calm myself, then read the blurb. An unnamed source in the San Antonio front office had reportedly expressed interest in signing "retired sharpshooter Tim Vilinski" for the final weeks of the regular season and the playoffs. That was it. One sentence.

My mind leapt to the possibilities. Maybe they wanted to spread the floor by adding a three-point shooter. Maybe they wanted a veteran defensive presence or a way to limit their young players' responsibilities and mistakes. I saw myself shaking hands with San Antonio's coach and claiming an NBA locker again. I felt the cool mesh of the jersey sliding over my face and settling on my shoulders. I heard the snap of a three-pointer plunging through the net and a whistle granting our bewildered opponents a timeout.

When I looked over at him, Matthew was staring at me. He blinked, then aimed his arm at something over my left shoulder. I turned to find a badly framed watercolor of a single potted flower.

"Painting," I said.

Then my cell phone started vibrating and Matthew pulled his arm back, startled and captivated by the rumble on the table.

The call was from Perry. "Did you see the *USA Today*?" he asked.

"Yeah," I said. "Can you believe it?"

"I think I know who the source is and I've got a call in

to him. They're not open for business yet down there. Will you play for the minimum, prorated?"

"Yes."

"OK. I'll see if I can get more but I won't push it."

"Tell them I've been working out."

"Have you?"

"No, but I'm in good enough shape to make them believe it."

"OK," Perry said. I could hear a smile in his voice. "I'll call you back."

When I flipped the phone closed, Matthew was staring at me again, as if waiting for my next move. I put my index finger in his palm and his hand closed around it. Though I had always appreciated that fans were paying their hard-earned money to attend our games, I had never played for them. If we had competed in empty high-school gyms, the games would have meant just as much to me. But the idea of playing in front of Matthew, even before he had any idea what he was watching, made the back of my throat tighten. I imagined walking from the floor to the sideline, looking up into the cheering crowd behind the San Antonio bench and finding him, my arena of one, a little bigger but still perched on his mother's arm, seeing me as I was for the first time.

On the way home, I called the office and told the receptionist I wouldn't be coming in. The idea of spending another day glad-handing farmers seemed ridiculous. I spent the rest of the walk wondering how I would convince Liz that even if Matthew remembered almost nothing of his next few months on earth, knowing that he had seen his father play in the NBA would mean something to him. When he was older, he would look up the box scores of the games he had attended and try to piece together my contribution from the raw statistics. Then he would imagine himself as a baby, distracted by the whistles and the shouts and the scoreboard lights, and catch a glimpse—maybe imagined, maybe real—of his father playing ball. He would know something more about me then, and maybe something more about himself.

Turning the corner onto our block, I was sure that Liz would understand—maybe not right away, but eventually—how important it was that Matthew see me play. These games would be different for her, too, in the same way they would be different for me: we would see them through Matthew's eyes.

As I pushed the stroller up the shallow incline of our driveway, I felt a vibration against my thigh. I pulled the phone from my pocket and flipped it open with one hand. "Hey," I said

"They were bluffing," Perry said.

I blinked. "What?"

"They wanted to light a fire under their guards so they went to a local beat writer with a story they thought would get their attention. They never expected the wires to pick it up."

With one hand still on the stroller handle, I turned and faced the street. "They said that?"

"No," Perry said. "They said they're very interested in working you out, in getting you in to talk to you. I said great, and asked them what their calendars looked like tomorrow. Then the guy mentioned a two-week timetable." Perry snorted. "If they signed you today, you'd have barely enough time to learn their system before the playoffs."

Perry gave me a chance to say something. I let it pass. Matthew, hidden beneath the stroller's canopy, made a chirping sound.

"A move like this is all about impulse," Perry continued. "It's a wake-up-one-morning-and-realize-we-don't-have-the-horses move. Nobody waits two weeks to do something like this."

"Yeah."

Matthew chirped again, louder this time. I walked around to the front of the stroller to find him with both hands in the air. With the phone pinned between my ear and my shoulder, I lifted him out of the stroller and braced him against my right hip.

"But the idea of bringing you back for the playoffs made the national news," Perry said. "Anyone who forgot you were out there will remember now."

I wondered if Perry remembered that he had used the same argument to cajole me into announcing my retirement.

"You there?" Perry asked.

"Yeah."

"You want me to follow up with a few teams?"

I could only shrug and shake my head.

"All right," Perry said. "I'll check in with you tomorrow and let you know what I hear."

"OK."

I flipped the phone shut and stared at it. "They were bluffing." As my mind worked its way around the implications of those words, I saw them on the phone and on the facades of the houses across the street, as if someone were projecting them wherever I looked. When I looked at Matthew, his eyebrows were twisted like dead caterpillars and wrinkles covered his forehead, but I could still read, "They were bluffing" on his face.

As I slid the phone back into my pocket, Matthew threw himself backward like a cliff diver. I clamped his calves against my ribs, but the weight of his head pulled them out before my free hand—not quick enough, not smart enough—could catch him. I dropped to my knees out of instinct, trying to get under him, but only increased his momentum. His head hit the cement first. His eyes jammed shut on impact and then opened wide, spinning a little, radiating horror and confusion. Then he screamed—a scream that stabs you because it says, "I'm hurt! Oh no, no! I'm really hurt!" I scooped him up and ran toward the front door, sliding my fingers over his head as I went. When I found a sticky knot on the crown, I was sickened and a little relieved—I had expected a dent or a crack.

As I kicked the door shut behind us, Matthew was pressing out the last of his breath in a few silent spasms. Then he filled his lungs and released another soul-splitting cry.

"What happened? What happened?" Liz shouted, running down the stairs.

"Matthew fell," I called.

I was putting ice in a plastic bag when she pulled him away from me. When she saw his crying face and swollen, bleeding head, Liz started to cry, too.

I handed the bag of ice to her and she held it on Matthew's head, whispering comfort into his ear between her own wracking sobs. When she looked at me, whatever she saw made her cry even harder.

"It's all right, Tim," Liz said. "It was an accident."

She meant that I hadn't intended to drop Matthew, that these things happen to even the most careful parents, and she was right. But nothing about Matthew's fall had felt like an accident. I understood then that Matthew would know me without ever seeing me play. He knew me already. And if my discontent—which I knew then I would never shake—had made my son throw himself to the ground, I wondered what else it would do to him.

DANCING MAN

When I was fourteen, I would lie in bed at night with foam-covered speakers over my ears and a dubbed copy of R.E.M.'s *Reckoning*—the band's second and best album—playing in my Walkman. For thirty-eight minutes, Peter Buck bounded between nimble arpeggios and syncopated strumming while bassist Mike Mills, freed from the duties of keeping time by Bill Berry's perfect drumming, played melodies and sang harmonies. And on just a couple of songs, for just a few notes, the cold, distant voice of Michael Stipe surged with warmth, grabbing me back from near sleep by some handle on my heart.

But the real revelation on *Reckoning*—my real reason for listening to it—was the piano playing. I kept thinking that the keyed acoustic chords, played with energy but without violence, would reduce R.E.M. to Elton John or Billy Joel or church musicians, but it never did. The music had an edge and, somehow, the piano parts didn't dull it. They made it sharper.

After seven or eight nights of making the album my bedtime story, I could play *Reckoning*—even the songs that had no piano—from start to finish on my mother's upright Steinway. The first time I played it straight through, I was a little surprised at what I had done, but I shouldn't have been. I had learned to play Reckoning the same way I had learned to play the minuets of Bach and Brahms: by listening.

Since the age of four, I had been trained in the Suzuki method, which requires its students to listen to recorded classical compositions until they can pick the notes out on the piano and play the songs from memory. By the time I was fifteen, if you gave me a tape, I could learn the songs on it in a hurry, and well enough to play them with some feeling. That ability—and the rehabbed Vox Continental organ I had inherited from an uncle—made me something of a commodity with Chicago bands while I was still in high school.

After graduation, I moved out of my parents' house and stayed with friends in the city, working odd jobs and playing out at local clubs almost every night of the week. I would play with any decent band—all I needed were a few hours with a tape of their songs, a fifty-dollar guarantee, and somebody with a car to fetch me and my organ for the gig.

By the time I had been out of high school for ten years, I had played nearly every club there was to play in Chicago. Every night I saw the same faces: the guy with the beard who recited poetry before the headliner; the beautiful, rough-looking woman who spent half the night fending off guitar players begging her to front their bands; the doughy biker in the black bandana who raised his two-finger rock salute and banged his head with eyes closed no matter what kind of music the band was playing. Chicago was a big town, but its live-music scene was small and incestuous. And if while making my way out after a show I passed one of these characters with my organ case in hand, he or she would invariably pat me on the shoulder and say, "Sounded great up there, man."

But we didn't always sound great up there. The bands I played with—the kind that hired an organ player just hours before their shows—were grossly under-rehearsed and, often, not particularly talented, but nobody seemed to care. Playing for the rock-club regulars in Chicago had become like playing the piano for my relatives when I was a kid: they couldn't bring themselves to tell me I had played badly, even when I knew I had. And if they couldn't tell me that I had played badly, how could their telling me I had played well mean anything?

I would have quit the whole live-music scene, but to make it as a full-time musician in Chicago, you had to play out as often as you could, whether you wanted to or not. Musicians in New York and L.A. could make a living playing recording sessions because big-budget acts made albums in those cities. In Chicago, where almost no one had a major-label deal, the most I'd ever gotten for playing on a recording was beer, pizza, and a ride home. Session work—the kind that didn't pay in food—was the sideman's Holy Grail. But to get into that world, you had to know somebody. I knew nobody that big.

My only way out of Chicago was to join a touring outfit. Out on the road, you had to win over people who had never heard you play before, then go to the next town and do it again. But getting out on tour wasn't easy. Not every touring band needed an organ player, and most that did already had one. And while I'd play a one-off in Chicago with anybody who could keep a beat and play three chords, any band I toured with would have to be pretty good—I had no interest in playing terribly in front of people who would have no problem telling us we were terrible.

One afternoon, I got a phone call at the place I was staying.

"Is this Dale?" the voice asked.

"Yeah," I said.

"This is Jamie Hyde. I front a band called Sod Off Shotgun." I hadn't heard of them. "I got your name from Ken Carson."

"Oh, sure," I answered. Ken was a singer-songwriter I had backed a few times at local street-festival gigs.

"My band is starting a twenty-date tour tonight at the Elbo Room. We've been together a while, and we rehearsed like hell for this tour, but now I'm worried our sound isn't big enough and I'm looking for an organ—Vox or Farfisa, something to shore up the top end."

I looked at the clock on the microwave: already seven p.m. I could probably learn the songs by showtime, but it would be tight.

"No problem," I said. "Should I come by for sound check? You can tell me what you have in mind for the organ parts, and I'll rehearse on my own until showtime."

"Oh no," he said. "I'm not asking you to play tonight. I'm inviting you to the show. If you like what you hear and have some ideas for organ parts, you can come out on the road with us."

It took me a moment to get that this guy was inviting

me on tour with his band. "What kind of stuff do you guys play?"

"Ska-rock," he said.

"Oh." I replied, a bit deflated. In my experience, fusion acts combined styles because they weren't good enough to play one straight.

"Just come to the show," he said. "If you want to play with us, meet me in the bar after the show. If you don't, leave."

Nothing about the call made me feel as if I'd found my ticket out of town, but I figured it was worth a walk to the Elbo Room to find out more. For a chance to get away from Chicago's rock-club regulars, I was willing to stand among them for an hour. Beats playing for them, I thought.

As I descended the stairs to the concrete bunker that was the Elbo Room, Sod Off Shotgun's gear was already set up on the small, slightly raised stage. I ordered a Jack and Coke at the bar at the back of the room and found a spot along its rounded edge where I could see the frontman's microphone through the forest of pillars holding up the ceiling. I sipped my drink, propped my elbows on the bar, and waited for Sod Off Shotgun to take the stage.

"Hey man," someone said.

The bandanna-wearing biker was standing next to me with a beer in his hand.

"Hey," I replied.

"You playing tonight?" He smiled maniacally and sipped his beer.

"No. Just listening."

"That's too bad." As Sod Off Shotgun took the stage

to perfunctory cheers, I felt the biker's heavy hand on my shoulder and the heat of his breath on my cheek. "You always sound great up there, man," he said, raising his voice over the lazy applause.

"Thanks," I said. But I didn't mean it.

Sod Off Shotgun got to work quickly. I didn't know much about ska, but the band seemed to have its basic elements down: a three-piece horn section that carried the melody when the singer didn't, a drummer and a bassist both locked into 4/4 time, and a guitarist who played only the upbeats. The sound was polished and sanitized, though—it lacked the grit that I thought ska was supposed to have. Whatever they were supposed to sound like, the guys in Sod Off Shotgun could play. They weren't fusing styles because they had to.

Jamie Hyde was a small man, much smaller than I'd expected, but he was a commanding presence. He leaned out over the stage's edge and growled lyrics at the audience, his brow wrinkled with effort and controlled menace, then turned toward the band, dragging his eyes over each member like an officer rallying his men to hold the line. And they did.

The more I listened, the more I decided that Jamie was right: the top-end of the band's sound was missing something. They needed an organ, and ideas for my parts came with as much ease—and excitement—as any ever had.

By the time Sod Off Shotgun left the Elbo Room stage to the applause they had earned, I believed that my days of settling for canned kind words from Chicago's rock-club regulars were over.

When Sod Off Shotgun went on, my organ and I held down the far right side of the stage, a few feet from the front edge. Behind me and to my left was the bass player, who rarely strayed from within a few feet of the drum kit. The horn section—trombone, tenor sax, and trumpet—stood in a row to the drummer's left. Jamie owned front and center.

As we played our first number each night, I would steal a glance at the faces in the audience. They often looked skeptical, and rightly so: the guys on stage—myself included—were wearing suits. Their skepticism only made me play harder—it was what I had left Chicago to face. By the time we were playing the last few songs of our set, however, heads would be bobbing in unison, and when we finished, the crowds of fifty or a hundred would whoop their appreciation and raise their plastic cups in the air. For two straight weeks, Sod Off Shotgun won over a new audience every night, and my playing was part of every victory.

An hour before we were scheduled to go on in Athens, Georgia, the band's roadie, Greg, told Jamie and me that he had left my organ in Tallahassee. The news shook me. I had inherited that organ from my uncle when I was fifteen, and I loved the feel of its almost weightless keys beneath my fingers and the distinctive whine-and-grind of the high E I always held down during sound check. Worst of all, if the organ was truly lost, I wouldn't have the money to replace it, and without an organ, what good was I to Sod Off Shotgun?

Jamie asked the local promoter if he knew anybody we could borrow an organ from, just for the night. The promoter left us alone in the tiny, humid greenroom and returned forty-five minutes later to tell us he'd come up empty. By then it was time to go on.

"Well, what should I do?" I asked Jamie.

He put his hands on his hips and thought for a moment. "Take the night off," he said. "We'll have your organ back by the time we play Raleigh."

My hands started to sweat. What if the band won the crowd over without me? Would Jamie sit me down after the show, say that he had been wrong about their needing an organ, and hand me a bus ticket back to Chicago?

As the band headed for the greenroom door, I spoke without thinking. "What if I just went out there and danced?"

Tom, the gangly, mustachioed trombonist, laughed as he walked out, but Jamie, who was always the last one out the door and the last one to take the stage, turned to look at me. I stood there in the gray suit the band's manager had bought me in Louisville, wondering if I looked as uncomfortable as I felt. On the other side of the greenroom wall, the lights went down and a few mocking whoops went up from the crowd. The sound of their skepticism sent a pang of desire through my stomach. "I could take my usual spot stage right and just dance." I shrugged. "Help get the crowd going."

Tom reappeared at the greenroom door. "Jamie, we're on, man," he said.

Jamie looked at him, then back at me. "Come on out," he said. "Let's see what happens."

Without an organ in front of me, I felt naked. I glanced at the horn section, envying them their gleaming brass instruments. Even Jamie had a microphone stand between him and the crowd.

To start us off, the drummer clicked his sticks three

times and hammered the snare. The rest of the band came in on his cymbal crash. I stood there for a moment, then remembered the deal I had struck to get on stage.

My dancing repertoire consisted of one move, a simplified version of an old hip-hop step called the Running Man. I hadn't done it in years, so I started tentatively, unsure how to hold my arms. Jamie glanced at me in the middle of the first verse then looked away, and it occurred to me that my small movements made it look like the band's music wasn't danceable. In a panic I made my movements larger, almost desperately so. If you can imagine a grown man repeatedly lifting his knees to waist level one at a time, and bringing one foot down to the floor at the same moment he slides the other foot out from under him, while jerking his arms up and down in unison like a toddler throwing a tantrum, you've got some idea of how I looked. I fixed my eyes on a neon Miller High Life sign on the club's back wall, but I could see people in the crowd pointing at me and laughing.

I started dancing again when the second song began, and this time, at least a half-dozen people, mostly younger kids in sweatshirts and plastic-frame glasses, joined in, doing their own versions of my only move. By the middle of the song, the number of dancers seemed to have doubled. Some of them were mocking me, but others looked like they had been liberated, as if they had been wanting to dance but hadn't felt that they could until now.

The band feasted on the crowd's energy. The drum and bass anchored us to the beat, and the horn section punctuated the melody with its blasts. Jamie was rocking the mike stand back and forth on its base, and moving his eyes around the room with a fierceness that seemed to sharpen the growl in his voice. To my ears, Sod Off Shotgun had never sounded better.

As the band played, I fought off thoughts of how ridiculous I looked and reminded myself that I was doing my part to win over a skeptical crowd, fighting the musician's good fight, and that, tomorrow night, I'd be fighting it as a musician once again.

After the show, Jamie found me in the greenroom, put his sweaty hands on my shoulders, and looked me in the eye. "How do you feel?"

"My feet are a little sore."

He clapped his hands on my shoulders. "Get a new pair of shoes in Raleigh."

"What about my organ?"

"Greg will get it back."

Greg did get it back, and he and his crew lugged it around for the rest of the tour. But they never put it on stage again.

When the tour was over, Jamie shook my hand, thanked me, and apologized if, with the dancing and all, things hadn't gone as I had hoped they would. I told him there was no need to apologize, thanked him for bringing me out on the road, and said that if he ever needed an organ player, he should give me a call. He said he would.

I was anxious to get back to being a sideman instead of a sideshow, so I went home to Chicago and put the word out that I was back in town. Soon I was playing six nights a week, wearing my favorite t-shirts and navy blue cut-offs instead of a suit and relishing the feel of my instrument: its sway on the rickety Z-frame stand, the easy give of the keys, the resistance of the gummy drawbar tracks.

To keep things interesting, I started manually adjusting the speed and depth of my organ's vibrato between songs. Whenever the guitarists took a few moments to tune down, I would lift the lid off my organ and manually adjust the trimmer pots, setting the vibrato to the levels I thought would work best in the next song. Chances were good that hardly anyone could hear the difference and, to my ears, the results were mixed. But when the adjustments worked, I felt almost as good as I had helping Sod Off Shotgun win over an audience of strangers.

An audience of strangers, however, was something Chicago still could not offer me. I was playing with the same bands for the same people—that bearded guy's poetry had gotten no better, and the bandanna-wearing biker was still giving set-long two-finger rock salutes to the musicians. But somehow, everything felt different. Maybe it was because I had been out on the road. Maybe it was because I was exploring new sounds with my instrument. Whatever the reason, despite all the sameness, playing in Chicago that winter didn't feel the same as it had before.

Then, all of a sudden, the sameness started to eat at me. Every note I played on the organ felt like an act of despair. Flat and sharp, syncopated and sustained—they all sounded the same. I did a weeklong residence at the Green Mill with a jazz combo and sat in during Happy Hour at a piano bar, but nothing I did changed anything.

One night in early April, during an undeserved encore with a local band, I held down a single note—a discordant C flat—for an entire song. When the song was over, the lead guitarist stared at me as I packed up my instrument. He was trying to look angry, but mostly he seemed hurt. Neither of us said a word.

As I headed for the club's door, carrying my organ case in one hand and the stand in the other, the bandana-wearing biker leaned out of a conversation he was having, tapped me on the shoulder and said, "Sounded great, man." He nodded once for emphasis before turning back to his conversation.

I stared at him. Then I hit him in the back of the knee with my organ case.

He grunted and fell to the floor. Holding his knee, he yelled, "What the fuck, man?"

Having sabotaged my ride's encore, I hailed a cab. The driver was about my age. He wore black, horn-rimmed glasses and a brimmed wool cap that mushroomed on the crown of his head. Strands of thick, straight brown hair covered his ears. The car stereo was tuned to the local college radio station, a favorite of Chicago music fans who had grown up on radio but outgrown corporate playlists. I had been a regular listener myself, but the nervous college-age DJs had started making me nervous with their hemming and hawing, so I'd gone back to listening to CDs.

As the cab turned left onto Western Avenue, I heard an energetic blast of horns and Jamie Hyde's growl coming from the speakers. I had never heard this song before—was it an old one that Sod Off Shotgun didn't play live anymore?

When the driver pulled up to the address I had given him, Jamie was singing the chorus after the second verse. I sat on the edge of the backseat and asked the driver, if he didn't mind, to wait. I figured it was worth the extra fifty cents to hear the song out. It wasn't every day I heard a band I had played with on the radio.

After the second time through the chorus, the organ solo began.

I inhaled sharply. The solo had been recorded on a Vox Continental—just like mine—and stuck pretty close to the melody line. But whoever had played it had added accents, little flicks of fifths and sevenths, and used the drawbars to silence a few notes of the solo's concluding, descending run. The performance was subtle, skillful, and just right for the song. I could have played a more difficult solo, but I could not have played a better one.

After the final cymbal crash faded, the boyish DJ ran down the list of bands that he had just played—Guided By Voices, Papas Fritas, Ween. "And that last track was a new one from Sod Off Shotgun, a song called 'Fundamental Physic.' Sod Off Shotgun will be in town next month at the Metro with Silkworm so, if you liked that song, or even if you didn't, head over to the Metro and check them out."

Jamie had written a new song with an organ solo. He'd recorded it and planned a tour.

And he hadn't called me.

I paid the driver and pulled my organ and its stand from the trunk of the cab. I stood in front of my friend's apartment for a few moments, then flipped open the latches of the case, took the organ in my hands, and hurled it against the crumbling brick façade of the three-flat, just above the main door. The organ fell to the ground drawbar-side first, bouncing once and spitting keys and transistor components around my feet.

I surveyed the destruction for a moment, kicking a couple of plastic pieces into the grass of the parkway. Then I walked into the three-flat's main door, leaving the stand, the case, and what was left of my instrument on the sidewalk.

As I trudged up the stairs, it hit me that I didn't have an organ anymore. And that, at least, was something different.

A few weeks later, the friend I was staying with shook me out of an afternoon nap on the couch and put the cordless phone in my face.

"Hello?" I said, still half asleep

"Dale. It's Jamie."

"Hey Jamie."

"How've you been, man?"

"Fine."

"Good," Jamie said. "So here's the deal. We're going out on the road again—"

"I heard."

Jamie paused. Maybe he had detected the edge in my voice. "You didn't hear about this," he said. "News just came down today. We're playing the festival circuit this summer. H.O.R.D.E., Lollapalooza, a few others."

"That's great," I said, taking care not to sound like I meant it.

"Yeah," Jamie continued. "Our single was used in a movie soundtrack, that got it on commercial radio, and the new album went gold last week."

"Wow."

"The movie's terrible. *Horn Balls*. Have you seen it?"

"No."

"Yeah. You're not exactly the demo. Basically, these kids in the high-school marching band start a ska band and become cool."

"Oh."

"Yeah. I mean, I appreciate what it's done for us but—it's a terrible movie. Anyway, the band's sounding tighter than ever—"

I actually winced when he said that.

"—but we've never played for twenty-thousand people before and I'm looking to stack the deck. I want you to come on the road this summer and dance like you did on our last tour."

As soon as Jamie had mentioned the festivals, I had begun to hope that he had decided to bring another organist on tour, or that the organist who had played on "Fundamental Physic" had been electrocuted or hit by a bus. I had never imagined he had called about the dancing. I said nothing.

"Look," Jamie said, "I know you'd rather be playing—and I think you're a hell of an organ player—but we need you to dance. Most of the crowd will be there to see some other band on the bill, and I don't want to be the act people skip to get a fucking henna tattoo. The dancing buys us time. While the crowd's watching you and maybe dancing along, we get a two- or three-song window to show them we can play. And right now that's all we need. You see what I mean?"

I did see. But I didn't want to say so.

"I can pay you three times what you made on the last tour and, if you want me to, I can try to get you some session work in L.A. this fall."

Session work. You had to know someone to get it, and Jamie was saying he would be that someone for me. I wanted to believe he could do it—as the frontman of a band with a gold record, he was the biggest music-industry figure I knew—but I wasn't sure he had the clout to drop an unknown into a paying session gig. "Do you think you can do that?"

"I think I can."

Those carefully chosen words sounded like "no" to me, and they made Jamie sound desperate. But was I any less desperate? I had destroyed my organ, and with it my only means of making a living. I had played only two gigs in the past six weeks, both on borrowed synthesizers that sounded like toys. I hadn't eaten yet that day, and given the rough way in which he'd shaken me awake, it seemed that I was wearing out my welcome at my friend's place. If I went out on the road with Jamie, I would get three meals a day and earn enough money to buy a new organ. Maybe Jamie would get me session work, maybe he wouldn't. But I would make sure he tried, and even if I moved to L.A. for a few months and played only live gigs, at least the regulars out there would be new to me.

"OK," I said. "I'll do it."

Jamie told me where to pick up my plane ticket and hung up. I pulled my gray suit off the floor of my friend's closet and borrowed ten dollars to have it dry cleaned. Walking down the stairs with the suit in a rumpled ball under my arm, it felt good to be doing something, and to have a plan.

I had almost reached the main door of the three-flat when I realized that, to make my plan happen, I would have to share a stage with the organist Jamie had chosen over me, and dance as if I were thrilled to do it.

I arrived at the Desert Sky Pavilion in Phoenix and gave the guard at the load-in area my name. He dragged his index finger slowly down the first page of the list on his clipboard, then flipped to the second and did the same thing. Halfway down the third page, his finger stopped and he waved me in. I exhaled and walked in the direction of the arrow on a wall-mounted sign that read "Backstage."

On my way to the greenroom, I ran into the drummer and bassist for Sod Off Shotgun and shook their hands. I felt a little awkward at first, but it was good to see those guys, and they seemed happy to see me. When I opened the greenroom door, Jamie and the horn section were inside.

Jamie got up immediately, shook my hand, and wrapped his free arm around my back. "Good to see you, man. Thanks for coming out."

"No problem," I said. The horn section kept their seats. I nodded to them. "Hey guys."

"Welcome back, twinkletoes," said Tom, the trombonist.

"Thanks, Horn Ball," I said.

Tom narrowed his eyes at me.

"Relax, fellas," Jamie said. "Get into your suit, Dale. We're on in twenty minutes."

Just outside the greenroom, I found a door labeled "Dressing Room C." I knocked twice, waited a moment for a response, and opened the door. Dressing Room C was a closet with a vanity. A row of light bulbs ran across the top of a mirror that was marred by a four-inch crack in the lower-left corner. On the shallow Formica counter, a steel-mesh cup held a blue pen, a mascara tube, and a pair of orange-handled fabric shears.

I hung my suit on a hook on the back of the door and got undressed. As I stood in my boxers and white socks with sweat prickling on my forehead and glistening in the yellow vanity light, I stared at the hanging suit and found that I just couldn't bring myself to put it on. The desert heat, the exchange with Tom, having to dance—all of it made me want to put on my own clothes, walk out of that closet, and disappear into the thousands assembled to see the show. But I didn't. Instead, I took the orange-handled shears, cut off the pant legs just below the knee, and got into what was left of my suit, hoping that with bare calves, white socks, and my usual shoes, I would feel just a little more like myself, even wearing a jacket and tie, even without my organ in front of me. Even dancing.

I found Sod Off Shotgun assembled in the wings, watching the emcee work the crowd with pot jokes. I assumed that the guy I didn't recognize was the new organist. No one bothered to introduce me. He was tall and had the easy good looks of a surfer, with curly, dirty blond hair, tanned skin, and a wide, toothy smile. And though he might have felt more at home in a pair of board shorts, he looked perfectly at ease in a suit. I envied him that, too. I was still eyeing my replacement—that's how I thought of him—when Jamie noticed my pants.

"Dale."

I looked at him, and the rest of the band looked back at me.

"What the fuck is this?" he asked, gesturing toward my bare legs, white socks, and green suede Vans.

"I'll be able to bring my knees up higher," I said. I

shrugged as if I thought the answer were obvious.

I could tell by the way he clenched his jaw that Jamie wasn't happy. But before he could say anything more, the emcee introduced the band, and Jamie waved the rest of us on ahead of him.

We went on to the half-hearted cheers of maybe fifteen thousand people, including those milling around on the lawn. The stage was bigger than any I had ever played on before. I took my place at the right edge, in front and a little to the right of my replacement.

When the band started playing, I started moving. From the first slide step, I paid little attention to how I felt or what I might have looked like. Instead, I focused on the sound of the organ. My replacement's monitor was right in front of me, and I heard every note he played. The subtle accents he added to the melody line confirmed that it had been him on the recording I had heard in the cab. And though I didn't quite believe my own ears, it seemed that he was varying the depth and speed of his vibrato during the song. How was he doing that without taking the organ's lid off and getting at the innards? I rotated ninety degrees—slowly, dancing all the way—and saw him turning something above the drawbars with the thumb and forefinger of his left hand while he played the keys with his right. Had he rigged knobs to the trimmers? Whatever he had done, he was changing the organ's vibrato on the fly, and with precision.

Even with all his talent and technological wizardry, my replacement never added anything that subtracted from the sound—he seemed to know how much was too much. As I rotated back toward the audience, I wondered where his organ was in the sound mix; could the crowd hear it as well as I could? I lifted my bare knees into the gleam of the stage lights, one after the other, over and over again, slowly gutting myself with a feeling I wanted to deny but couldn't: I hoped nobody was missing a note of this guy's playing.

While I wondered what they could or couldn't hear, the kids in the crowd showed me what they could see. Out on the lawn beyond the assigned pavilion seats, several hundred were dancing by their blankets. During the third song of the set, a group of dancers gathered in the aisle directly in front of me. Security tried to shoo them away at first, but the kids kept coming and when the beefy, yellow-shirted guards saw that all they had in mind was dancing, they let them be. The dancing kids pointed at me and waved, as if they wanted me to acknowledge them. I just kept moving, watching them out of the corner of my eye and wondering what I could possibly mean to them.

The crowd swelled continuously during the fifty-minute set, and by the end there were only a few hundred empty seats in the pavilion. Sod Off Shotgun played an encore—no other supporting act played one that day—and left the stage to a roar that dwarfed the half-hearted cheers that had welcomed them.

After the set, the band gathered in the greenroom. Everyone seemed to feel pretty good about the performance and, despite my role, I felt all right, too—good enough, in fact, to introduce myself to my replacement.

"Hey man," he said. "Tyson Jakes."

"Good to meet you," I said. We nodded at each other for a moment as I worked up the determination to say what needed to be said next. "You sounded great today. Your monitor was right in front of me and, you know, I liked what I heard."

He smiled broadly. "Thanks, man. I'm just trying to get by out there, really. I mean, the tunes are new to me, and these guys have been together for a while. They're tight. I'm just trying not to stick out like a sore thumb, you know?"

I heard Tyson asking for a musician's empathy, and I gratefully gave him mine. "I do," I said. "But you fit in really well."

"Well, I hope so."

To be addressed this way—as a musician, as an equal—felt like recognition of who I really was, a recognition no one else in this band had made since Athens. Between his humble, easy-going nature and his chops on the organ, my replacement was proving difficult to hate.

"Well, I'm going to change out of this suit," I said. I think I actually clapped him on the shoulder. "I'll see you on the bus."

As I made for the greenroom door, Tyson yelled out, "I got to tell you, man. I love watching you dance." At that, the other conversations in the room petered out. Feeling the eyes of the rest of the band on me, I smiled to show Tyson that he didn't owe me a compliment, that the one I had paid him had been freely given. I opened the door to leave, hoping he would leave well enough alone.

"It really gets the crowd going," Tyson continued, "and that makes things so much easier for the musicians."

I heard Tom the trombonist snicker as I closed the door behind me. Even then, I knew that Tyson's remark had been innocently made. Surely no one had told him that I played organ, and that I had played for this very band. But innocent or not, from the moment he said "for the musicians" as if I weren't one, hating Tyson Jakes was easy.

As the tour continued, Sod Off Shotgun won over bigger and bigger audiences, and my dancing was a big reason why. No organ player could have carried the crowds the way I did. From the very first song of the band's set, thousands of kids mirrored my movements. If I let my arms dangle at my side or swabbed my sweaty forehead with my forearm, they did, too. Once, when I raised my palms in the air during a drum solo, thousands of hands suddenly appeared in unison above the heads in the crowd.

Nobody in the band said anything to me about the crowd's devotion—I'm not entirely sure anyone else noticed it besides me. Even so, I started to worry that Jamie would think that I was trying to show up the band. So, when we played in Oklahoma City, instead of facing the audience as I danced, I faced the musicians, pointing myself where the crowd's attention was due: toward Jamie when he was singing, toward the other guys—even Tyson—during their solos. When I checked the crowd at various points during the show, they were watching the band instead of me.

From then on, the dancing kids did what I did and watched what I watched, but I didn't understand why until we played a festival outside of Kansas City. I was facing the trumpet player during a solo and glanced at the crowd to find—as by then I expected to—that the dancing kids were focused on him. Squinting into the middle distance, the trumpet player picked his spots in and around the scales, departing from them at just the right moments with just the right notes. I marveled at his range and imagined matching him note for note on the organ, hitting the keys in rapid succession like a one-handed typist.

That was when I realized why the kids had latched onto me. While few of them would ever have the chops to match the trumpet player's solo on any instrument, almost all of them could dance as well as I could. That made me the shortest path to seeing themselves on stage. In the eyes of the dancing kids, I was them—so far as they could tell, there was nothing I could do that they couldn't. And after every set, I left the stage to their cheers, wishing I'd had a chance to show them otherwise.

We were drinking bourbon and beer backstage after our final show of the tour when Jamie came out of the greenroom. "Fellas," he said, "we've got one more show to do."

"What?" Tom the trombonist said.

The drummer lowered himself to the cement floor and sat Indian style with his beer between his legs. My heart dropped with him. Just twenty minutes ago, I had waved to the cheering crowd and run off stage toward what I hoped lay ahead for me: Los Angeles, a lovingly rehabbed organ, and—with any luck—some session work. But the linchpin of that plan had other plans for me.

"Mercury Rev was scheduled to play a support slot at a Tibetan Freedom gig outside Denver tomorrow. They canceled to go out on their own tour, and the label asked us to step in for them. As much as possible, I want the label feeling like they owe us one, so I said we'd do it. It's for charity, so we're not being paid, but I got the label to match your per diems and pay for any travel rearrangements you have to make. Nobody goes in the hole on this one. If you do, let me know." He looked at his wristwatch. "We leave in two hours. I'll see you on the bus."

The trumpet player swore under his breath, and the bassist smiled at Jamie's retreating figure with anger in his eyes. Nobody liked the idea of playing for free at the end of a long tour, but nobody argued, either. Jamie had spoken.

As Jamie walked away, Tom yelled out, "Who are we opening for?"

Jamie kept walking, but looked back over his shoulder and raised his voice over the muffled vocals bleeding in from the pavilion. "R.E.M."

I blinked, trying to get my head around what Jamie had just told us: we were opening for R.E.M. Just when I had had that realization long enough to start enjoying it, I remembered that I would have to dance again tomorrow, and that R.E.M. would have every opportunity to watch me.

I had one thought on my mind as I joined Sod Off Shotgun in the wings before our set: please, please don't let R.E.M. see this. I looked across the stage for any sign of them in the opposite wings—they were empty. Behind me a bald stagehand was securing a ragged curtain to a brick wall, but there was no sign of the headliners. I hoped that they had decided to boycott the flavor-of-the-month ska-rock band the label had stuck them with, or that they had been poisoned by the buffet and were taking turns heaving into the green-room toilet. Whatever the case, I didn't want R.E.M anywhere near the stage until they were ready to take it.

Then another thought occurred to me—once I went on, I would have no idea who was standing in the darkness of the wings. Michael Stipe could watch my every move—my only move—without my knowing he was there.

The house lights went down and Sod Off Shotgun went on. I moved with big, bold motions from the first note, hoping that everyone—both in the audience and backstage—would think that my dancing was ironic, a joke that we were all in on. Halfway through the first song, however, I realized that nobody in the audience was getting the message because no one was watching us. Traffic in the aisles of the theater was constant, and more people were heading for the lobby than returning from it. I counted at least twenty people standing with their backs to the stage, talking to friends in the row behind their own. In the third row, two girls had their heads down over a magazine. Jamie thundered away at the audience with all the menace he could muster, leaning forward over the faces in the front rows and back to connect with the eyes in the balcony, and the band played fast and tight behind him, nailing the notes and keeping perfect time. But no one was bothering to watch.

After the third song of the set, Jamie told the band to play "Fundamental Physic," which was usually our closer. Hoping to make Jamie's gamble pay off, I dropped the ironic body language and started dancing like hell, but the audience still wasn't paying any attention. Nothing we did could compete with "Free Tibet" pamphlets, shouted conversations, and the lure of R.E.M. merchandise for sale in the lobby.

The scene could have pleased me—after a summer of winning over festival crowds with my help, Sod Off Shotgun was being taken down a peg by a crowd of indifferent R.E.M. fans. But I wasn't pleased—I was confused and a little angry. Why weren't these kids looking at me? Why weren't they dancing?

During the next song, I left my position at stage right and danced toward the center of the stage, thrusting my palms in the air and screaming, "Come on!" to the crowd. A few dozen people looked up and cheered my outburst, but that wasn't enough for me. So I pointed at groups of uninterested chatters until the kids around them tapped them on the shoulders and they turned toward the stage. I kept pointing until almost everyone in the crowd was watching me.

As I migrated back to my usual position on stage, the eyes of the audience stayed on me. No one was dancing, but everyone was watching the dancer now. I faced the crowd, basking for just a moment in their attention. Then I turned and dutifully faced Jamie as he sang. That, I thought, should do it.

But when I checked the crowd a minute later, the kids were still looking at me. I held out my right arm and pointed at Jamie until my shoulder began to burn, but pointing did no good—I couldn't direct their eyes where I wanted them. And no matter what I tried, I couldn't get anyone to dance.

When the set was finally over, Jamie threw down the microphone stand and stalked off stage. I followed without waving goodbye to the crowd. From the moment I entered the wings, I scanned for any sign of R.E.M. but, to my relief, I saw only stagehands and roadies.

Jamie stood near the back wall of our dressing room and stared into a mirror, seething. In the overhead fluorescent light, the rest of the band looked pale and exhausted. I felt for them. They were good musicians who had played a charity show and been treated shabbily by the audience.

That was no way to end what had been a successful tour.

As we stood around in silence, I began to worry that the band might blame me for the way the set had gone. What if they thought that everything I'd done had been a vengeful grab at the spotlight? What if, instead of setting me up for session work, Jamie vowed to do everything in his power to ensure that I would never work in L.A.? But I had pointed at him. I had tried to shift the attention where it belonged. Then I remembered that no one knew I had been directing the eyeballs of the audience for the past few weeks. All Jamie and the band knew for certain was that their shows had been going great until the dancer started pointing and waving his arms and moving all over the stage.

Suddenly, I was too anxious to be in the same room with the rest of them. I threw my suit jacket in the corner, grabbed a bottle of water, and headed for the door. As I opened the door, Jamie said my name. I looked over my shoulder at him, holding the doorknob in my right hand. He was still standing in front of the mirror, but he was staring at the ground now, supporting his weight with his fists on the Formica counter. Without lifting his eyes, he said, "You did everything you could."

I nodded and closed the door behind me. Jamie had said the right thing—but I wasn't sure he had meant what he had said.

I roamed the backstage passageways in my untucked button-down and cut-off suit pants, occasionally flattening myself against a wall to avoid being bowled over by beefy, sweaty members of R.E.M.'s road crew as they hustled between the load-in area and the stage. I felt a little lost now that the tour was over. I tried to focus on what lie ahead, but when I envisioned arriving in L.A.—even with money in my pocket and an organ—the possibility of building the life I wanted seemed, at best, remote.

I turned down a long, narrow corridor directly behind the stage and plunged into relative darkness. The only light was a yellow bulb in a socket high on the wall at the passage's middle point. The moment my eyes adjusted, I saw an egg-shaped head silhouetted against the light of the load-in area beyond. I knew immediately who it was.

We entered the bulb's glow from opposite directions. His cheeks were pockmarked and darkened by stubble. Glitter at the outer corner of his left eye caught the faint yellow light. His thin green sweater had been stretched into shapelessness.

He was almost past me when, emboldened by the dim lighting, I touched his elbow. "Excuse me," I said.

Michael Stipe recoiled slightly, pulling his elbow against his side, and walked a few more steps before stopping.

"I just wanted to say that *Reckoning* is one of my favorite albums, and that I really like what you do. It's an honor being on the same bill with you."

He looked at me for a moment. "Who are you with?" he asked, quietly.

"Oh," I said. "Sod Off Shotgun."

He blinked and nodded. "And what do you play for them?"

If he had asked, "what do you play?" I would have said organ right away. But that wasn't what he had asked. I knew then that he had watched our set from the wings, and that he had seen me dance. As I stood there in the faint light, my mouth forming words I couldn't speak, Michael

Stipe walked away.

I hurried back toward the relative safety of Sod Off Shotgun's greenroom and made it without humiliating myself any further. When I burst through the door, Sod Off Shotgun's horn and rhythm sections were gone. A tall, balding man wearing a loose silk shirt, dark jeans and black boots was stooped over Jamie, talking to him. Tyson stood next to Jamie with an arm across his stomach, working the edge of his thumbnail between his front teeth.

"The whole point of these shows is to road test their new material," the man said, "and it's built around keyboards. They can play all older stuff if they have to, but they don't want to." He looked at Tyson. "Just the first eight songs. The new songs. That's it. They'll take it from there. "

"I thought Mills played keyboards," Jamie said.

"On the albums," the man said. "Live, he plays bass."

"And where's their touring player?"

"The airport. His wife and daughter were in a car accident."

"Right," Jamie said. "You said that."

The man looked at Tyson again. "So what do you say?"

"When do you want to go on?" Tyson asked, wincing.

The man checked his watch. "An hour from now at the latest," he said.

That's when I realized that the guy was R.E.M.'s road manager.

Tyson shook his head. "If you wanted a guy to play the right chords in the background, I could do it. But eight new songs built around keyboards? In an hour?" Tyson held up his hands as if being mugged. "I'm sorry, man. I'd love to, but I can't help you."

"That's too bad," the road manager said. He stared at Tyson, trying to shame him into playing.

Jamie lifted his index finger in my direction. "This guy might be able to help you."

The road manager looked at me, then looked back at Jamie with a pained expression. He must have seen our set, too.

"He started out playing organ for us," Jamie continued. "I gave him a tape and he learned our set overnight."

"He won't have that long this time."

"I'm telling you," Jamie said, "the guy can play. He'd still be playing for us if we hadn't lost his organ and found out what his dancing did for us."

I didn't look at Tyson, but it occurred to me that he was probably learning for the first time that I played the same instrument he did.

The road manager stared at me, biting his upper lip. "If I got you a CD of R.E.M.'s new material," he said, "could you learn the keyboard parts in an hour?"

I didn't want to play—not after what had happened with Stipe. But I wouldn't deny that I could. "Yes," I said.

The road manager nodded at Jamie and started walking toward the door. "Thanks for your help."

"No problem," Jamie said.

The road manager put his fingertips in the middle of my back and guided me out the door ahead of him. "Where are your pants?" he asked.

"I might have a pair on the bus."

"Forget it," he said. "Come on."

I followed him through the corridors to R.E.M.'s dressing room. He opened the door and told me to wait outside. Then he closed the door behind him. A few moments later, he emerged with a Discman and a pair of headphones. Handing them to me, he said, "They'll play the first eight songs on this disc in order. The last song has a keyboard solo. If you don't want it, tell me before you go on stage."

"OK," I said.

The road manager's forehead was beaded with sweat. "Don't go too far," he said. "We're on in fifty minutes."

That I would be onstage behind a keyboard for the first time in weeks—in less than an hour—playing songs I had just learned—with R.E.M.—on the same day I had embarrassed myself—twice—in front of Michael Stipe—presented more potential disaster than I could process. Luckily, I didn't have any time to try. I sat down beside a concrete pillar and started listening. I played the first track. Then I listened to it again, fingering notes on an imaginary keyboard. When it was over, I moved on to the second song and listened to it twice.

By the time I had made it through the first seven songs, I had heard a Moog, a Mellotron and a Farfisa. Two of the songs featured four measures of synthesizer in the clear before the rest of the band joined in. The last song on the disc—the one with the keyboard solo—was an up-tempo rocker that sounded more like Reckoning-era R.E.M. than any of the other songs. The solo was compelling and relatively simple, and I knew as soon as I had heard it that, when the time came, I would play it.

As I was listening to the eighth song for a second time, the road manager nudged my foot with his own. "Let's go," he said.

He headed for the stage and I followed him.

"Does the band know I'm playing with them?" I asked.

He didn't respond.

We were about ten steps from the wings when he suddenly ran ahead of me and shouted, "OK, you're on!"

By the time I reached him, the house lights were down and the crowd was screaming. "Where are the keyboards?" I yelled.

"In the back, stage left," he said.

Taking small, careful steps across the darkened stage, I headed toward a tubular bulb hovering in the blackness at the far side. When I reached the light, I found that it illuminated one side of a three-sided bank of keyboards. I surveyed the various instruments at my disposal, running my hand gently over the playing surfaces. I had played each of the instruments before, but had never seen all of them in one place outside of a store.

Inside the keyboard fortress I felt protected, but isolated. I was ten feet to the left of the drummer—the one who'd replaced Bill Berry after his retirement—and five feet behind him. Fans in the fifth row were closer to the front of the stage than I was.

Suddenly, white spotlights ignited above each member of the band and the crowd's roar intensified. Except for the light from the tiny hooded bulb, I remained in the dark. Apparently, I hadn't needed to hide behind that pillar—R.E.M.'s road manager was doing everything he could to ensure that the band never saw me.

The drummer counted off the first song and I came in on cue. Having missed sound check, I was relieved to find that I could hear the synthesizer in my monitor. I hoped I could hear the rest of the keyboards just as well. I was nervous, but by the second chorus of the first song, I felt the music loosening me up.

R.E.M. had probably recorded the new songs one track at a time over a few weeks, with each member showing up at his appointed time and recording his parts alone, his band mates present only in the playback in his headphones. Now, on stage, that piecemeal process was over and R.E.M. was a musical whole. When Buck went for texture on the guitar, Mills played the melody on bass, and the two of them kept time when the drummer took a fill. Stipe phrased his lyrics in and around the gaps they left, and not a single word or note felt out of place. As I listened, the music they made shepherded my hands to the right backing chords and single-note chirps. I believed that their playing rendered me incapable of making a mistake, and that belief freed me to pour some feeling into the songs.

Then, during the synthesizer-only opening of the fourth song, I made a mistake. I played Em-C-G-F instead of Am-C-G-F, but I didn't realize I had botched the chord progression until the rest of the band came in and Mills yanked me back in line with an exaggerated pull on his A string. I got the message, but the attempt to slip me onstage without the band noticing had been foiled.

After the second chorus, during Buck's solo, Stipe walked off the stage. My eyes followed his slouching silhouette into the wings, where he found the road manager and began rolling his finger—he never quite pointed—at the taller man. The manager held his palms up, probably apologizing and asking what else he could have done. Stipe waved him off and retook the stage at a run, reaching the mike just in time to sing the third verse.

The mistake gutted me. Never mind that I hadn't had much time to learn the songs. Never mind that the slip-up was certainly lost on an audience hearing the tune for the first time. I had messed up and I knew it and R.E.M. knew it. That was enough.

I played the next two songs mistake-free but without any energy. The drummer—still the new guy, until I had showed up—caught my eye and tried bucking me up with a nod, but I wouldn't have it. After the sixth song, Stipe introduced the band: the drummer first, then Buck and Mills, each of whom got an extended ovation. Then he started the next song with eight bars of a cappella vocals. I was grateful to have been excluded.

After the seventh song of the set, I felt an inkling of relief—I had one more song to play before I could escape into the wings, and by the time R.E.M. finished their encore, I would be long gone. That relief evaporated when I recalled that the remaining song called for a synthesizer solo. I stared into the wings, desperate to make out the shape of the road manager, hoping it wasn't too late to tell him that I didn't want the solo, that Buck could take it on guitar, or that we could go right into the chorus from the bridge. I was still squinting into the off-stage darkness when I heard the drummer's sticks click together once, twice, three times, four. The blood rushed out of my stomach, I pressed out a B flat on the keyboard, and suddenly my solo was one measure closer than it had been.

I locked my fingers in shallow, crooked arcs to keep them from shaking. My terror increased as I failed to push out of my mind how badly I needed this solo to work. Jamie may or may not have had the power to blackball me from session work in L.A., but I was certain that Michael Stipe could ensure that I never so much as taught piano lessons.

The drummer had set a breakneck pace, but Stipe and the band were up to it and they dragged me along. I pounded my foot to the beat, trying to give the tension in my hands a way out, but by the second time through the chorus my fingers ached at the joints.

Then it was time, stiff fingers or not. I felt the unexpected heat of a light above me and heard the soundman move the synthesizer toward the front of the mix. I stuck closely to the solo I had heard on the CD at first, then added some left hand on the upbeat. I thought that the syncopation would add a little texture, but it did more than that. In my monitor I heard two different solos—one that blended sustained notes and nimble runs and followed the downbeat, and another that punched on the upbeat like a ska guitar. To my ear, either solo would have worked on its own; together, they were somehow greater than the sum of their parts.

I looked up for a split second—Mills had turned to face me and was nodding his head and stomping the heel of his right boot to the rapid-fire rhythm. The crowd got louder as my solo neared its close and started clapping with the beat. The band matched the energy of the audience, and I did everything I could to match the band.

When I finished, the light went off overhead, and I returned to playing sustained chords behind the guitar and bass. The drummer kept us in lockstep time despite playing increasingly more complicated fills. Sweat flew out against the light each time he hit the snare. Mills, still pounding his boot heel against the stage, had turned to face the crowd again, and Stipe was captivating the kids in a way I never had. Thousands of arms stretched out toward him.

We drove the song to its peak. When it ended with a powerful drum flurry, the crowd erupted into screams. As the roar poured into my ears and chest, the song's beat—bass-snare-bass-snare-crash-snare-bass-snare—kicked up again in my head. Suddenly I could feel it in my arms and I started clapping—hard claps for the bass, harder ones for the snare—in perfect four-four time.

Just as the crowd's sustained roar was beginning to weaken, I left my keyboard bank and stood in front of the drummer, clapping out the time he had kept with such precision. But he only looked over my head at Stipe, so I walked into the cone of light that shone down on Buck and appealed to the crowd, clapping with my hands above my head. The kids in the audience recognized me and started cheering even more raucously. A few of them jumped high into the air over and over again. After all, if I was up on stage with R.E.M., then so, in their own minds, were they.

I had carried the beat on my own for thirty seconds or so when a dozen kids near the front of the stage realized that I was not simply applauding them. They started clapping and, after a few beats, the kids right behind them joined in. The clapping spread visibly through the crowd. As it reached the balcony, the drummer started hammering out the beat, and Mills and Buck followed him into a reprise of the coda. I stood at the front of the stage, my hands my only instrument, serving once again as the bridge between musicians and their audience.

And then I started to dance, a frantic, ecstatic interpretation of my signature move. The kids roared again, and some of them started dancing, too. As their claps reverberated through my body, I closed my eyes and tilted my head back, absorbing their energy with pride and humility.

When I opened my eyes, I realized that I had danced within a few feet of Stipe. He stared at me, unmoving. Then he turned his back on me and faced the crowd at stage right. Raising his hands above his head, he, too, started clapping on the beat, leading the kids, taking them in, for just a moment, as a part of his band. And as I danced at the front of Michael Stipe's stage, I imagined that some part of him was clapping for me.

ACKNOWLEDGMENTS

The following enriched my imagination of the stories in this book: Gerald Nachman's *Seriously Funny*; Joe Garner's *Made You Laugh!;* "Abe Lincoln vs. Madison Avenue," the masterwork by Bob Newhart that is described in "Captive Audience;" "Donald Trump is Done to a Turn," written by Jesse McKinley for *The New York Times*; "A Night In With: Abe Vigoda; Only as Old as You Act, " written by Linda Lee for *The New York Times*; Abe Vigoda's self-authored Carnival Barker audition piece, a few words of which were included in Linda Lee's piece for the *Times* and paraphrased in "In Memoriam;" "Alan King a Model for Seinfeld, Crystal," written by Peter Ephross for *The Jewish Journal*; "Comedian, Actor Alan King Dies at 76," an *Associated Press* report published at redOrbit.com; The Oral Cancer Foundation's bio of Alan King, where I found the fantastic joke that King wrote about his mother (it appears in "In Memoriam"); *The Godfather*, a film by Francis Ford Coppola—a few lines from the screenplay, written by Mario Puzo and Coppola, appear in "In Memoriam;" the Abe

Vigoda entries on Biography.com and TCM.com; the James Caan biography at filmreference.com; season two, episode ten of *Dinner for Five*, on which James Caan appeared as a guest; the now defunct (so far as I can tell) AbeWatch website; "Comedy Central Presents: The N.Y. Friar's Club Roast of Drew Carey;" The Internet Movie Database at imdb.com; "Won't Get Fooled Again," a story by Jim Shepard; Kim Cooper's book N*eutral Milk Hotel's In the Aeroplane Over the Sea*; *6 colors, 1,800 pulls, 2 dogs*, a short film by Anthony Vitagliano and Coudal Partners; the poster art of Jay Ryan of The Bird Machine; the poster art of Daniel MacAdam of Crosshair Silkscreen Design; *On Avery Island* by Neutral Milk Hotel; *Make It Through The Summer,* an EP by the Chamber Strings; *Reckoning* and *Up* by R.E.M.; "The Impression That I Get" by the Mighty Mighty Bosstones; "Love Will Keep Us Together," performed by Captain and Tennille, written by Howard Greenfield and Neil Sedaka; "Faithfully" by Journey; Cheap Trick's *At Budokan*; "Do You Feel Like We Do?" by Peter Frampton and Cream's "White Room."

Many people met my desire to be a writer with encouragement and respect long before I had any book to show them. In particular, I thank my teachers: David Leavitt, Jill Ciment, Padgett Powell and Mary Robison, as well as Brandy Kershner, Susan Hegeman, Benedict Giamo, Ron Weber, Sr. Ricardo, Mr. Kane, Mr. Stracco, Mrs. Lia and Linda Schuster Brown.

Thanks also to Kevin Guilfoile, Scott Turow, Jim Shepard, Eileen Pollack and Charles D'Ambrosio for their support, and to Robert Lasner and Elizabeth Clementson for working to turn my manuscript into a book. And my gratitude to Kathy Snow for proofreading an advance copy of the collection.

Finally, thanks to my friends and my family for seeing me through with their love.